The hooded man aime

Ian lunged at the man, ramming into him to at least throw off his aim. Gunfire resounded in his ears. The weapon went off before he could stop it.

Cold, brutal waves washed over them as he fought the attacker. A fist filled Ian's vision. Pain radiated across his face. Salt water washed into his nose and burned.

Ian shoved the man down in the wet sand and pinned the man's arms behind his back. But the ocean gripped them both. Ian floundered as the current ripped the man from him and pulled Ian under. He held his breath, trying to gain his footing again. He met the sand on his knees, broken shells cutting into his flesh as he gasped and choked on water. Hands gripped him, and he wrestled someone to the ground.

Too late he recognized the feminine form beneath him. "Jonna!"

"We have to get out of here. It's too dangerous!" she yelled.

Elizabeth Goddard is the award-winning author of more than thirty novels and novellas. A 2011 Carol Award winner, she was a double finalist in the 2016 Daphne du Maurier Award for Excellence in Mystery/Suspense, and a 2016 Carol Award finalist. Elizabeth graduated with a computer science degree and worked in high-level software sales before retiring to write full-time.

Books by Elizabeth Goddard

Love Inspired Suspense

Coldwater Bay Intrigue

Thread of Revenge
Stormy Haven

Texas Ranger Holidays

Texas Christmas Defender

Wilderness, Inc.

Targeted for Murder
Undercover Protector
False Security
Wilderness Reunion

Mountain Cove

Buried
Untraceable
Backfire
Submerged
Tailspin
Deception

Visit the Author Profile page at Harlequin.com.

STORMY HAVEN

ELIZABETH GODDARD

HARLEQUIN® LOVE INSPIRED® SUSPENSE

Recycling programs
for this product may
not exist in your area.

LOVE INSPIRED BOOKS

ISBN-13: 978-1-335-49059-9

Stormy Haven

www.Harlequin.com

Printed in U.S.A.

For in the time of trouble he shall hide me in his pavilion:
in the secret of his tabernacle shall he hide me;
he shall set me up upon a rock.
—Psalms 27:5

Dedicated to my Lord and Savior, Jesus Christ.
You're the King of my heart.

Acknowledgments

Thank you to all my writing buddies for your encouragement through the years on this long writing road. It's been an adventure, to be sure. And special thanks goes to my family—thank you for putting up with me while I get lost in my writing world. I couldn't do this without you. Elizabeth Mazer—I'm so grateful for the opportunities you've given me to write for you. To my agent, Steve Laube, thank you for seeing something in me, for believing in me.

ONE

Only three more miles...

Rain pelted Jonna Strand as she jogged the wintry Washington shoreline. Her cheeks grew numb from the wet cold as white vapor clouds puffed out of her burning lungs.

But as focused as she was on her run, a subtle alarm snaked up her spine.

She'd learned long ago to pay attention to that sixth sense that forewarned of danger. The alarm going off now had nothing at all to do with the storm that had advanced from far out in the Pacific faster than meteorologists had predicted, catching Jonna off guard.

She remained on high alert—a souvenir from her previous training as an ICE agent. More specifically an HSI special agent—the Homeland Security Investigations division of Immigration and Customs Enforcement. She'd put that life behind her, but the training remained.

Jogging six miles every day, she made an effort to stay as fit as she'd been while in law enforcement, the job she'd left three years ago. Even brutal winter storms couldn't keep her inside. Except weathermen had predicted this system would wreak havoc *and* threaten lives—so maybe she should have stayed inside, especially given that her instincts warned another possible threat loomed.

Up on the ridge overlooking the beach, a man jogged, keeping pace with her. Only a crazy person would be out in this storm. She could almost laugh at that.

But she felt something was off.

Jonna shoved the apprehension aside and focused on her jog. She'd know soon enough if her instincts were right.

God, please let me be wrong.

Just two more miles…

Then she'd reach the Oceanview Lodge, where she and her guests could watch the wind, rain and waves buffet the coast.

Her business thrived on the winter weather drama that drew people from all over the country. Since the lodge perched on a bluff overlooking a rocky section of the beach, her clients were protected from the hazards posed by seriously high waves as they dashed magnificently against rocky outcroppings, or crashed into the beach.

Like today's storm that threatened high winds, twenty-foot waves and a significant surge in sea level. Citizens of the town of Windsurf had placed warning signs on the beach about the dangers of sneaker waves and ocean swells. Jonna had assisted in the placement of the signs, and she should have been back before the brunt of the storm hit. No matter. She would be okay as long as she kept clear of the sneaker waves.

Never turn your back on the water.

Never turn your back on the past.

The foreboding thought caught her by surprise. In

coming back to Washington, she'd tried to do just that. So far, it had worked.

Far from the threats of her past career, she'd found a sense of peace here in Windsurf on the Pacific side of Coldwater Bay. A few small towns bordered the bay and a peninsula separated them from the ocean.

With her training and her trustworthy Sig Sauer P320 Compact, which she had affectionately named Max, she could take care of herself while she enjoyed managing this peaceful lodge—a stormy haven where she could watch the storms from a safe distance.

The inclement weather wouldn't prevent her from running.

And neither would a stalker. Was her follower the man who'd already abducted and murdered five women along the Washington coast over the last six months? The Shoreline Killer?

If so, then he'd just picked the wrong woman to mess with.

Or was it someone from her past? Her old boss in Miami, Gil Reeves, had contacted her not long ago—to catch up, he'd said. See how she was doing. Then he'd casually mentioned her name had come up in intel chatter. He'd been giving her a heads-up.

It had been three years since she left. Why would anyone care to talk about her, much less find her, then follow her here? She was no threat to any criminal operations these days. There was no reason to attack her and bring an investigation down on themselves.

A violent gust caused her to misstep, but she righted herself and second-guessed her decision to run outside no matter the weather. A wave could wash up and sweep her away, rip her off the beach and take her out into the depths. Or it could wash over her, carrying driftwood that could knock her unconscious.

Either scenario would result in her death.

She had to get back to the safety of the lodge, but another part of her wanted to face off with man on the ridge pacing her.

Except she hadn't brought Max. So better to head straight home, where she could arm herself.

She was almost there.

Just beyond the rocky outcropping ahead of her, rustic steps led up to her lodge on the ridge.

Dark, angry clouds bled into an equally dark ocean, blurring the line where sky met sea. The breakers rolled in, reached higher and crashed harder. Jonna stayed just out of reach, her breaths coming faster as she ran on the wet sand, her running shoes leaving footprints that quickly melted away.

Salty ocean spray lashed at her, taunting her. The ocean swelled. Her heart hammered as she ran. If she could make it back to the lodge and grab her gun, then she could find the guy and get some answers.

Fear and determination fueled her steps.

Dread surged as a wave towered up and arched over— a sea monster opening its mouth wide, baring ugly sharp teeth ready to chomp down and consume her whole. Jonna barely escaped.

When she glanced over her shoulder at the ridge, the guy was gone. She was alone in the storm after all.

He hadn't followed.

Had her instincts been wrong? Was she that rusty?

Relief surged as she neared the lodge. She waited until the crashing waves subsided so she could make her way around the rocks.

A gust of wind forced cold into her marrow, despite her rain-resistant cold-weather jogging garb. Running today had been the absolute worst idea.

Before another wave crashed forward and the ocean surged, blocking her path, Jonna had to get past those rocks.

The hooded man stepped around them and aimed a gun at her.

Ian Brady was too late.

He lunged at the man with the gun pointed at Jonna, ramming into him to at least throw off his aim. Gunfire resounded in his ears. The weapon went off before he could stop it.

Cold, brutal waves washed over them as he fought the man and disarmed him. Thankfully, the receding waves whisked the gun away. A fist filled his vision. Pain radiated across his face. Salt water washed into his nose and burned.

Ian drew from his experience and training to ignore the pain. He shoved the attacker down in the wet sand and pinned his arms behind his back, then lugged him to his feet. He had the man securely contained in his grip. Now to haul him off to the sheriff.

Except Ian was fighting another assailant now. The Pacific gripped them both. Ian floundered as the current ripped the man from his grasp. Tossed him. Icy cold water pulled Ian under. He held his breath, trying to gain his footing again. He met the sand on his knees, broken shells cutting into his flesh as he gasped and choked water. Hands gripped him, and he wrestled someone to the ground.

Too late he recognized the feminine form beneath

him. "Jonna!" The woman who ran the lodge where he stayed.

And the woman Ian had been sent to secretly protect.

"We have to get out of here—it's too dangerous," she yelled over the cacophonous storm.

Now *she* was trying to protect *him*?

He pulled her to her feet. Together they ran away from the angry ocean to the stairway that climbed the cliffside and carefully maneuvered the slippery steps to the landing. They stopped beneath the shelter of her lodge's terrace. Driving winds and lashing rain accosted them even under the covered porch. At least they weren't still on the beach. Below, the ocean boiled and waves collided with rocks and blasted the shoreline.

In the distance, Jonna's would-be killer crawled onto the beach. At first he floundered when another wave tried to take him, then he found his footing and fled. The guy was too fortunate. He was also too far up the beach for Ian to give chase, but he couldn't just let the man get away so easily. On the landing of the steps, Ian watched the shooter head for another set of stairs up the cliff to make his escape from the raging waves. Ian started to run after him, but Jonna grabbed his arm.

Surprised at the strength in her grip, he turned to face her.

"Come on." Turmoil lingered behind her brown eyes as her gaze pled with him. "Let me get you inside."

Jonna acted like the protector here—her law-enforcement background coming through.

"No. He tried to shoot you. I want to catch him and find out who he is. Maybe I can get to him if I take my car."

Her lips hardened in a flat line as she lifted her chin. "We'll take mine."

She guided him around the lodge to a single-car parking garage. They entered to find her silver GMC Terrain and climbed into the unlocked vehicle. She quickly fished the keys from the visor.

The wind rattled the structure. "Are you sure this is a good idea?" he asked. "You could stay here while I search for him." Ian had only meant to protect her, but he had realized his mistake too late. Still… "The guy tried to kill you, Jonna. Not me. It's safer if you stay here." Plus, she'd just finished a six-mile jog and her energy could very well be spent, but he knew to say no more.

Starting the ignition, she sent him a tempered glare. Wouldn't do to glare at a guest, but Ian had insulted her.

Jonna backed from the garage, then took off down the street. She probably wanted to speed, but rain plastered the windshield, rendering the wipers useless.

"Careful now. I don't know how you can see anything."

"I'm being careful. I know my way around. You look for the guy while I drive." The hint of a bite edged her tone.

Clearly, Jonna didn't like being coddled. Ian focused on searching for the man. Had he gotten into a vehicle and left the area already? Had someone been waiting for him in a getaway car? If the storm would ease up, maybe he could actually see something, but he had a feeling their efforts were futile. His face throbbed from the punch, and his body ached from the damp cold that soaked through him as he sat dripping in her vehicle.

As if finally realizing it was cold, Jonna flipped on

the heat. Chilled air flayed him. It would take a few minutes for it to warm up. Ian almost regretted her move.

"We weren't that far behind him. I hope he didn't get away." He scanned the cars parked in the street and the few driving the road despite the sheets of rain. "Why did the guy try to shoot you?"

He tossed the words out to get her talking. Ian had been sent to protect her from a possible attack, but he wasn't certain she knew she was being targeted. And even if she did, she wouldn't expect *him* to know about it. She didn't know why he was here, which made his task more difficult.

Her long, dark hair plastered to her head, she glanced his way intermittently. Droplets clung to her pale face. Even drenched she was drop-dead gorgeous.

"I don't know. But he was pacing me up on the ridge while I jogged the beach."

Guilt suffused him that she'd been running alone without him there to keep watch until it was nearly too late. He'd assumed she wouldn't jog today. The old adage about assumptions came to mind. But that wasn't good enough. She could have died today, and that would be another failure. Another life he'd cost.

"You're usually out jogging the beach too," she said. "Where were you this morning? Not afraid of a little rain, were you?"

"No, not a little rain. But I read the warning signs and they deterred me. I wasn't going to jog in the storm. Why did you?" He really wanted to know the answer to that. He needed to understand her better if he was going to protect her.

"I trusted the weather app I use to tell me when the dangerous part of the storm system would hit. According to the meteorologists, I had a couple of hours to jog. That strategy has worked well enough for me until today."

"You could have been swept away. There's no surviving those violent waters."

"I run a storm-watching inn, don't you think I know that?" she asked. "No need to worry about me."

"Maybe we should jog together from now on, if we don't catch this guy right now." He'd offered earlier to jog with her, but she'd insisted she needed the time alone since she ran a lodge. So he'd given her the space. If she suspected Ian had an agenda, she didn't show it.

He watched out the window to see if he could catch a glimpse of the guy. Indecision roiled in his gut. Hired by his uncle Gil, the Special Agent in Charge of the Department of Homeland Security's Miami field office, Ian was here to watch over Jonna. Uncle Gil had been Jonna's boss, and even though she'd left HSI, he still felt an obligation to keep her safe. Especially from the criminals she'd angered in her years of service. He'd made it clear he didn't want Jonna to know Ian had been sent.

Like most law-enforcement officers, Jonna would believe she could take care of herself—after all, she'd been trained to do so—and she would send Ian away. Or worse—she'd hightail it back to Miami, furious that someone had come to Washington to find her. Uncle Gil didn't want Jonna back in Florida. He'd hired Ian to watch and report if he saw anything suspicious, as well as protect Jonna if necessary.

According to Uncle Gil, three years ago, Jonna had just finished wrapping up a human-trafficking-ring case when she went missing. The department feared she was dead, but then she called Gil and explained she'd been attacked and left to die in a marsh. The guy probably thought he'd succeeded in killing her.

She'd woken up in a hospital in a small town off the Florida coast and walked out before she answered their questions. She didn't have the answers they were looking for—she didn't know who had shot her or why. The injury, the whole experience of lying there in the marsh and waiting to die, had been too traumatic. In order to cope, her mind had buried those memories out of her reach.

She resigned over the phone. Gil managed to keep the information out of the media. As far as the man who'd shot her knew, she was dead, that is, if he even questioned or came asking. But recently her name had popped up via an informant—and Gil was worried she would be targeted again.

What could she know that would make her a target?

"I wonder if it's the Shoreline Killer," she said. "I need to call the sheriff."

"Let's say it wasn't the Shoreline Killer. Could it have been a disgruntled guest?"

Jonna quirked her face. "Are you kidding me?"

Ian stifled a laugh. "Look, I'm not saying there's actually anything to complain about at your lodge. Not at all. But didn't anyone ever tell you that you can't please all the people all the time? Just humor me. Could someone have been unhappy?"

"Enough to try to kill me? No."

Ian didn't think so either but he had to ask. "Any acquaintances outside of the lodge, then? Or…" *Is there anyone from your past with a grudge?* Ian couldn't say that or he'd give himself away.

"What's with the questions? You sound like a detective."

Maybe he already *had* given himself away.

"Just a concerned guest, that's all." And while his motives were more complex than that, he really was concerned. When Ian had learned that Jonna had gone jogging, he'd rushed out and down the landing steps to join her, even in the storm. That's when he'd spotted a man watching her from behind the rocks.

A man with a gun.

A man who seemed to have made a clean getaway. Ian didn't see the shooter anywhere. How could he in this storm? Trees swayed and rain rippled like sheets in the wind. The guy had likely escaped in a vehicle and was long gone.

"Thank you for your concern, but there's no need." She sighed and glanced around the interior. "Like I said, we should call the sheriff. I need to find my phone. I hope it survived."

"You don't have a waterproof cell? I'd think that would be a priority for someone who lives here." He sent her a wry grin and tugged his own phone out from a protective pocket. "Let's see. Looks like my waterproof cell really is waterproof. Let me give the authorities a call and tell them what happened."

"Okay, fine. I'll head back. But I don't need emergency vehicles showing up at the lodge. I don't want my guests to worry or be afraid."

"Then you can be glad the shooter picked a location on the other side of those rocks. Your guests probably didn't see a thing." What if Ian hadn't gone after her? His gut tensed.

He'd failed to protect before. He couldn't let that happen again—had left that life behind so he wouldn't find himself in this position. He wouldn't even be here trying if Uncle Gil hadn't needed someone he could trust. Ian hoped he didn't let the man down. Or that he didn't let Jonna down, though she had no idea why he was here.

She drove down Main Street in Windsurf while he focused on his cell and called the sheriff's department to relay the message about the shooter. Someone would meet them at the Oceanview Lodge in short order.

She steered into her garage and closed the door behind them, muting the sound of the winter storm. The call made, he remained sitting in the GMC, wrestling with how much to tell her.

Indecision and exhaustion weighed on Ian. "We should get back inside and get out of these cold wet clothes. We need to be ready for the authorities when they get here."

Covering her eyes with her hands, she nodded, then quickly dropped them. Flashed him a tenuous look. "Thanks, Mr. Brady. I should already have thanked you. You saved my life."

"I know you like all your guests to call you Jonna so it's not so formal, but then you keep the formality on your end. How about you call me Ian instead? I'd prefer it, actually."

Ian and Jonna had spent plenty of evenings sitting near the big roaring fireplace in the common area and talking well into the night along with other guests. Still, she'd kept the formality with him, just like she did with all her customers, calling them by their surnames. It went hand in hand with her insistence that she could take care of herself, her determination to keep her distance from others and not let anyone near. Couldn't reveal any weakness. He understood that mentality. That's why when he looked at Jonna, he could see right through the tough veneer she projected to the soft side she hid away—a side he very much wanted to know more about, against his better judgment.

Ian didn't mind the extra barrier between them. He wasn't sure why he'd removed it now.

"I like to keep the lines drawn so there's no confusion." Her brow wrinkled, and she held his gaze for a bit longer than necessary. "All right, Ian. You saved my life on the beach today. I owe you."

"I think we're even, considering you pulled me out of the water before the ocean took me."

Though she shot him a soft smile, a tempest brewed in her eyes. "You wouldn't have been caught in those waves if you hadn't been trying to save me. I don't want to put any of my guests in danger. And I don't want them to panic either, so I hope you won't mention this to them if they didn't see it for themselves until it's determined they could also be at risk."

"I won't mention it. But once someone from the sheriff's department arrives the rumors will fly."

"True. I guess we'll see what happens." Her brow furrowed. "If it's the Shoreline Killer, the guests should be told what happened for their own safety. I'll let the sheriff decide if the guests should be informed." She faced him, her caramel-brown eyes taking him in. "While I'm grateful for your help, you should know that normally I can take care of myself. It was a lapse on my part. I'll be more careful next time."

She got out of her Terrain.

Ian slowly opened the door and climbed out too. While Jonna might believe she could take care of herself, all that tactical training and situational awareness could only go so far when a vendetta became personal. Ian had learned that the hard way.

He didn't doubt her capabilities, but everyone needed someone to watch their back now and then.

Especially if the man who thought he'd killed her in Florida had come for her again.

Now he better understood Uncle Gil's directive that he should hang around to watch over her without letting her know he was her secret bodyguard.

TWO

Jonna hadn't missed Ian's skill in taking the man down. He'd been ready to march the man right up the beach and call the authorities—she'd seen it in the determined stance of his shoulders and the resolve on his rugged features. And he'd nearly succeeded. Did he have a military background?

But the ocean had had different plans for both men, tossing them like they were nothing more than driftwood. Fear for Ian's life had corded her neck. She couldn't let the ocean take him, and had willingly risked her own life to pull him out before it was too late. Nothing heroic on her part—just a balancing of the scales. She owed him for saving her. He hadn't hesitated going after the guy to protect her, and without his quick action, she might be dead now.

She needed to be more alert. More prepared. From now on, she'd jog with her Sig, Max, like she should have to begin with. In fact, she'd take Max everywhere.

Aware Ian studied her, Jonna led him to the door that connected her garage to the main lodge, hoping she could escape to her own private cabin on the south side of the structure without encountering her guests. A short enclosed walkway connected the cabin to the lodge, for which she was grateful, especially on an occasion like this when she was chilled to the bone, but she wished they would have connected the garage to her cabin as well. To enter through her private entrance outside the lodge, she'd have to go out into the storm again.

Hands trembling, she accidentally dropped her keys on the concrete floor.

Ian snatched them up, beating her to it, and handed them over. Their fingers brushed.

His blue eyes had grown dark and piercing, more gray like the storm outside. "Are you okay?"

The intensity of his gaze unsettled her and she hesitated before responding. "As soon as I get out of these wet clothes I'll be better."

"Same here. Let's meet in the common area after we change," he said. "We can wait for the sheriff's department together."

She nodded her agreement. "The deputy in the Windsurf Substation can get here faster than someone coming from the county sheriff's department, which is just under an hour away, even if the storm slows him down a little. Unless he's assisting someone else, which could very well be the case in this weather."

Ian on her heels, she hurried through the door, wanting to retreat before he could see just how the incident on the beach had shaken her. The adrenaline was beginning to crash. Not good. She had to hold it together for a few more hours.

Inside the lodge, she could see her guests clinging to big mugs of coffee or hot chocolate and enjoying baked goods. Her employees often baked up muffins, or they purchased breakfast foods from the restaurant next door to the lodge for those guests who didn't want to venture out into the storm to eat at the restaurant for a bigger menu.

Everyone was focused on the panoramic windows overlooking the storm's wrath and nature's spectacular display.

Good, she could slip away and gather her composure.

Before she turned the corner that led to the short walkway to her cabin, Ian touched her arm. She hesitated, then slowed but kept her back to him. Couldn't he just go to his room and change? Leave her be?

"Someone just tried to kill you. Be careful, Jonna. I'm worried about you."

"You don't expect me to find an attacker in my room, do you?" She'd teased, but the possibility corded her throat with a measure of fear.

Ridiculous. She shrugged off the apprehension.

"I could check it for you first." His voice held genuine concern.

If only that didn't warm her to her toes. She turned to face him and tossed him an easy smile, hoping she could hide her fear. "You don't have to worry about me. I can—"

"I know. You can take care of yourself."

He'd finished the sentence for her, but she read all too easily the doubt in his searching blue eyes. And what he didn't say.

The guy had gotten away. If he had targeted her specifically, he could come back and attack again at any time. Who was he? Was it the Shoreline Killer? Or maybe the man who'd shot and left her for dead in Miami?

If it was the man from Miami, would she recognize him if she saw him, considering that much of what happened had been lost in the recesses of her mind? Some of her memories of that incident were as clear as Ian standing before her now. But she couldn't remember the face of the man who had shot her.

Maybe…maybe it had nothing at all to do with what happened in Miami, and the man on the beach this morning really had been the Shoreline Killer.

Ian had saved her today. Protection poured off of him. She had the sudden urge to go to Ian and let him wrap his arms around her. To be held and comforted and protected. But Jonna shoved the unbidden thoughts away and stood taller. She walked backward, willing herself to want nothing more than to feel the door to her cabin— her safe haven—against her back.

"I'll meet you ten minutes in front of the fireplace, okay?"

"See you then." He waited until she'd walked the rest of the length of the enclosure and opened and closed her door.

Jonna snuck a glance through the peephole. He lingered a few more seconds and then disappeared around the corner.

Pressing her back against the door, she calmed her pounding heart. She rushed to the side table and opened the drawer. Withdrew Max, then searched her cabin just to be sure she was alone. Chop Suey, her big tabby cat—a Maine Coon—snoozed on the top of the maroon thrift-shop armchair next to the window, without a care in the world, oblivious to the tension rolling through Jonna.

She wanted to collapse on the sofa. Too much had happened in the last hour, not the least of which was one of her guests turning out to be a hero.

He'd booked a room in the main lodge a little over a

week ago, and since then, she'd found herself looking at him now and again. Taking in his strong features and lithe physique. His thick, mussed black hair that hugged his collar. She'd imagined running her fingers through that hair, and then scolded herself for the silly fantasy. She shouldn't have these entirely too-personal thoughts. She couldn't allow herself the luxury of a relationship. But she kept wondering if there was a Mrs. Brady. Or if he waited here, expecting a close friend to show up. She shouldn't be having those kinds of thoughts about one of her guests.

She learned her lesson a couple of years after Aunt Debby had bought the lodge—a fixer-upper—as an investment. She'd hired Jonna to run the place, keeping her niece's name out of the paperwork for now. Peter was the contractor who'd helped renovate and restore the building.

She could easily have fallen for Peter. He was handsome. Charming. Clearly interested in her. Maybe she'd still been vulnerable after what she'd endured. Peter had been there to comfort her and…he'd asked too many questions about her life and her past. He'd only wanted to get to know her better, but she didn't want to revisit the ugliness in Miami. Her reluctance to answer his questions had frustrated and then angered him as he demanded to know what she was hiding. The relationship that could have been fell apart quickly after that. And so she'd put Peter behind her, just like she'd put behind her everything that had happened in Miami.

She got up and peeked through the mini blinds and out the window to make sure the man hadn't made his way back. The storm still raged outside. Maybe that would deter him for a while.

She settled at the kitchen table and thought back to her messed-up life.

If she couldn't share all of her life with Peter, then she had no business letting the relationship go deeper.

Nothing had changed. She was still too broken, and could never truly let herself be vulnerable enough to love or be loved.

And now with this attack on her life, she realized she could never let down her guard. Trouble seemed to find her one way or another.

She'd endangered a guest today, but she was grateful he'd stepped into the fray.

Since Ian had checked in at her lodge, they'd forged a laid-back friendship, neither of them sharing too much about themselves. Just enough to make conversation and still hold everything close. At least that had been her intention, and she sensed he was no different.

While his friendship had been just right—exactly what she'd needed, she feared that if given too much leeway, her heart could easily step across the line she'd drawn. Somehow she had to keep her heart from betraying her.

Enough of these thoughts! Someone from the sheriff's department could already be here.

After donning warm slacks, a floral T-shirt and soft sweater, she quickly towel dried her hair. It would have to do. She put on blush and lipstick, then paused as she stared at herself. She hardly ever used makeup unless it was a special occasion where she was dressed to impress.

What am I doing? Some part of her had wanted to look good for Ian, but that was ridiculous. She absolutely wasn't going there with him or anyone. She couldn't afford to.

Jonna exited her cabin and entered the lodge, fireflies dancing in her stomach at not only meeting Ian again, but also facing the substation deputy, Ollie Shane. Or would Sheriff Garrison himself show up? That would depend on where he was in the county when the call came through.

She hurried around the corner to the large living area comfortably decorated and boasting a massive fireplace and panoramic window. A few guests lingered, their attention drawn to something outside—storm watching. The reason they came to Oceanview Lodge.

Jonna didn't see Ian. She breathed a sigh of relief and planted a smile for the benefit of the guests, but as she neared the window to face the storm, she realized what had garnered their attention. It wasn't the storm after all, but the two men standing on the landing of the steps to the right down below them.

Wearing a weatherproof jacket, Ian stood with Sheriff Garrison near the edge of the awning, barely safe from the wind and rain. So the sheriff himself had come to investigate. Ian gestured with his hands, apparently sharing the events of the last hour without her. Why were they outside, though? Had Ian been showing the sheriff the rocks where it all happened?

She wanted to share her side of the story but didn't want to go back out into the storm.

"Jonna, what's going on?" DiAnn Morrison, one of her employees and a good friend, approached. "Why's the sheriff here?"

Jonna urged DiAnn down the hall toward the kitchen. Only employees used it so she didn't have to worry about a guest overhearing her words. She didn't want to alarm anyone, not until she'd spoken to the sheriff, but DiAnn should know. "A man tried to shoot me on the beach."

DiAnn took a step back, sheer terror in her eyes. "What did you say?"

Jonna didn't repeat herself but simply waited, allowing DiAnn to absorb the news.

"I can't believe it. That's just horrible."

"Please keep all of this to yourself," Jonna urged. "At least let me speak to the sheriff first and see how he wants to handle it."

"You don't think it's that...that serial killer, do you?"

"I don't know. Be on the lookout for anything or anyone suspicious."

DiAnn eased into a chair. Jonna would leave her to compose herself. Once she'd calmed down, she'd be able to calmly divert any questions the guests might have. DiAnn would know to maintain the bright and cheery demeanor that kept the guests coming back every year. She left DiAnn and grabbed a jacket on the hook by the kitchen door, then braved the storm again. Wind and rain lambasted her as she made her way around and found the two men behind a protective barrier that blunted the storm's effects.

"And why were *you* there on the beach?"

At the question aimed toward Ian, Jonna hesitated revealing herself. She wanted to hear the answer to that, unfettered by her presence. She hadn't even considered the question of why Ian had been on the beach, which meant her skills were getting rusty.

Ian had caught a glimpse of Jonna before she ducked out of sight. He shivered. "Could we talk about this someplace warm?"

"I think any evidence left behind is long gone, so

there's no reason to dig around out here. Let's get inside," Sheriff Garrison said.

Ian gestured for them to head back toward the lodge. Jonna stepped out at that moment. "Sheriff Garrison, thanks for coming."

"Under the circumstances, I can't say I'm glad to be here. Are you all right?"

"I've been better," she said. "Let's go inside and grab something warm to drink while we chat in the kitchen. If you don't mind, I don't want to worry my guests, so I haven't yet shared with them what happened."

Ian and Sheriff Garrison followed Jonna into the lodge and then the kitchen. Ian gladly shrugged out of the jacket, hung it on a peg at the door and rubbed his hands together. He would've much preferred to have this conversation near the big roaring fire, but other guests would hear their discussion.

"I'll make you some coffee or hot chocolate," Jonna said. "Which would you prefer?" She ushered Ian to a chair at the table, and the sheriff joined them.

Sheriff Garrison shrugged out of his jacket too. "Coffee's good."

Jonna sent Ian an acknowledging glance—she already knew his preference.

"You were just about to tell me why you were on the beach when there are warning signs about this storm."

Ian stiffened. "I usually jog every day. Just ask Jonna. But I had decided to avoid it this morning because of the storm—" he eyed Jonna "—and because of the signs. Then I heard one of the guests mention they'd seen Jonna going for a run and they were worried about her since the storm was moving in faster than expected. The waves had grown bigger."

The sheriff scrutinized him as if trying to figure out if Ian had some special interest in Jonna. Ian kept it cool.

"So you took it on yourself to check on her."

He shrugged. "Why wouldn't I? Seemed like the right thing to do." *There. Try to make something out of that.* "I'd gone to the landing to see if she was close by and that's when I spotted someone suspicious over behind the rocks."

"Suspicious, how? And why would you decide to confront a man who looked suspicious rather than calling 9-1-1?"

Really? There'd been no time! "He pulled a gun. And he was aiming it at Jonna. What would you have done?"

"You told me that part. And you're right, I would have taken action." The sheriff still scrutinized Ian. He would probably run a background check on him. Ian hadn't broken any laws, so he wouldn't worry about it. But he wasn't sure he wanted the man to know the kind of security he'd worked. At least not yet.

"Ian was a hero today, Sheriff. He saved my life. Now, don't you want to hear my side of the story?" Jonna turned and handed the sheriff and Ian cups of coffee, then crossed her arms, watching Ian, studying. She didn't miss a thing, this one. But she'd tried to divert the sheriff's undue attention from Ian.

"Sure. Go ahead."

"I saw a guy up on the cliff, keeping pace with me. It was only unusual because of the storm. Only a crazy person would jog in this. So I noticed him."

Ian shared a look with the sheriff, then stared at Jonna.

Jonna pursed her lips. "Don't look at me like that."

"So you're a committed runner. Continue with your story," Sheriff Garrison said.

"I suspected he was up to no good. When the guy disappeared I figured I was just being paranoid. Still, I couldn't wait to get out of the storm. The waves were coming in hard and fast and I could get trapped on the beach. Then the man stepped out from behind the rocks and pointed a gun at me. That's when Ian tackled him. He got a bloody nose for his heroic efforts," she added.

The sheriff's sharp gaze shot up from his pad and paper. "The guy you believed was pacing you on the ledge, are you sure it was the same man who tried to shoot you?"

"I'm pretty sure. He had on the same hoodie. No one else was out there." Her gaze flicked to Ian.

The sheriff scratched his chin, then eyed them both. "There can't be too many joggers out here in this kind of weather in the winter, so it's possible someone else noticed him too, but did either of you get a good look?"

"With the wind, rain and sea spray, it was a blur for me," Ian said. "His hood covered his face, but I'd say five-eleven, muscular build. Pasty white skin and dark hair."

"That's a pretty good description for it being a blur," the sheriff said.

Ian hoped he and the man weren't going to have a problem. He'd talk to Uncle Gil about it first, but maybe he should pull the sheriff aside and tell him the real reason he was here. It would mean sharing about Jonna's past—that is, if she didn't fess up herself. Maybe the sheriff already knew.

"What about you, Jonna? Can you add anything or do you disagree?"

"When he pointed the gun at me," Jonna said, "I looked at him long and hard. But it was from a distance and the storm had picked up, so I couldn't see him very clearly. I think Ian's description is right."

"We'll get you two down to the station to look at some photos. Maybe we can get a forensic artist in too."

"Do you think it could be the Shoreline Killer?" she asked.

Creases grew around the sheriff's eyes and mouth. "I think it's too soon to say. But I have to ask you, Jonna—can you think of any reason someone would want to kill you?"

Ian resisted the urge to hold his breath. Now, there was a loaded question. Would Jonna tell the sheriff about her past career in Miami? It was clear he didn't already know or he would be bringing that up now. Ian looked forward to hearing her answer.

The sheriff glanced his way. "Mind if I speak with Jonna alone, Mr. Brady?"

"Of course not." Ian scooted from the chair. "I'll just be waiting by the fire if you need me for anything else."

Ian left the room. At first, he hung near the door hoping to hear what Jonna would say, but DiAnn came around the corner. Ian nodded, smiled and headed to the main room to watch the storm through the window and stand by the fire. Instantly, the guests gathered around him to question him about what was going on.

Uncertain how much either the sheriff or Jonna wanted him to say, Ian begged off and headed to his room. He needed to call Uncle Gil anyway. Uncle Gil needed to know about what happened today. Maybe he would release Ian to be forthcoming, though the more he found out about the woman, the more he understood his uncle's reasons for sending someone to watch over her—from a distance.

It would help if his uncle had more details to share about that old case in Miami, but Jonna hadn't known who had shot and left her for dead. Amnesia. Too bad. For all they knew the same guy had shown up on the beach today.

Ian hated not knowing whom he was up against in protecting a woman who didn't want protection. Her survival could depend on it. But this wasn't the first time he was expected to protect someone against an unknown enemy. Except he'd failed before.

God, please don't let me fail this time.

THREE

Utter darkness pressed down on Jonna as she lay in bed, tossing and turning. Doing everything except sleeping. The storm should pass in a few hours only to be followed by another. In the meantime, the howling wind brought to mind images of ghouls. She didn't believe in those, of course, but goosebumps still rose on her flesh. That probably had more to do with the fact that every time she closed her eyes she saw the man pointing a weapon at her today. Then her thoughts immediately shifted to her past. She'd worked hard to forget the scattered, broken memories she had about what happened in Miami, but the events of today brought those distorted, gruesome images rushing back.

She felt the excruciating pain of a bullet in her abdomen as she lay in the shallow part of a marsh where someone had dumped her, slowly bleeding out. She moved in and out of consciousness—the sun bore down on her, baking her alive. Flies swarmed as though she were already dead. How much longer before an alligator or some other predator found her?

All of the pain was unforgettable, but the face of her shooter had disappeared into a dark corner of her mind.

Enough!

She pushed the sheets off and got dressed, then found her flashlight in case the power went off, which was more than likely in this stream of storms.

The guests had been adequately warned and were prepared for a power outage, and they'd also been informed about Jonna's attack. The sheriff had advised them to be cautious and aware of their surroundings. Most of them already were, considering the Shoreline Killer. In addition, her guests were outraged on Jonna's behalf.

It was well past midnight when she made her way to the expansive living area and found Ian by the fireplace, stoking the embers. She wasn't surprised to see him. He'd brought them back to life, the orange glow of the flames bouncing off his sturdy form. He stared at the fire, his expression troubled.

Jonna momentarily averted her gaze to the windows, but only darkness stared back through the panoramic glass as an eerie wail threatened to keep her guests shivering and awake in their rooms. She wasn't worried about complaints from the guests come morning. It was all part of the package—the reason they kept coming back every year. For the thrill of it.

As she watched Ian and the blazing hearth, Jonna let herself listen to the crashing waves pounding the shore— they were like past mistakes beating her soul.

Earlier in the day, the sheriff had taken both her and Ian into the substation at Windsurf to look at mug shots online, an exercise that had sent a throbbing pulse of tension, anxiety and pain straight through her brain.

And it hadn't let up all day, even when they'd come back, and she'd busied herself with her chores at the lodge while questions about who had tried to kill her today consumed her thoughts.

There was a chance it was connected to her past, in which case she should contact Gil, but she wasn't ready to talk to him yet. She didn't want the nightmare to have followed her here. Why couldn't she live in peace here in Washington?

She felt like her life was beginning to unravel.

Again.

Fortunately, she had employees—DiAnn, Lisa and Kelsey—who were amazing with the guests and seemed to love the lodge as much as Jonna. No matter what she had to deal with in her personal life, she knew she could count on them to keep the lodge running smoothly. They were a real Godsend. She didn't know what she would do without them, especially now.

The sheriff believed that women's lives could be at greater risk if Jonna's attacker was the serial killer who'd already taken five women along the coast. Her situation would certainly fit the serial killer's pattern—the victims had all been out jogging the beach when they were abducted and killed. From now on, Jonna would carry Max with her everywhere. Living in Windsurf, she'd slowly allowed herself to pretend everyone could be trusted and that she was completely safe. She'd wanted to forget her life in Miami ever existed, but it wasn't to be. Cold reality had slapped her in the face when the man pointed a weapon at her and fired, searing the image on her mind to go with the trauma from Miami.

Twin images now impressed in her mind—the most recent one sharp, while the old one was frustratingly fractured.

And into that clear picture stepped Ian—all muscle,

strength and sharp, able-bodied moves—to save the day. Save her life.

That image also lingered in her thoughts all day.

She hung back watching him now as he finished stoking the flames in the massive fireplace, his jaw working as if he were as disturbed as Jonna. Finally, he eased his chin up and lifted his gaze to meet hers.

He'd known she was there?

Of course, he would. After what she'd seen today, she knew the man was trained to be aware of his surroundings. She had to find out about that training.

The other guests were asleep, or *trying* to sleep in this storm. She approached Ian, a thousand questions spinning through her mind. Questions she'd had to keep to herself all day in the presence of the sheriff or deputies or guests.

But now they were alone. Truly alone.

"Something bothering you?" he asked like he didn't have a care in the world.

Yes! Yes, there's something bothering me. She steadied her breathing as she drew near, but not too near. Not too close to this man. "I have a few questions for you."

He jerked his head back slightly. Oh, yes. Now she had his attention.

"Ask away. I'll answer if I can."

She would have preferred if he'd said he had nothing to hide.

He replaced the poker. Stuck his hands in his pocket and leaned against the wall near the fireplace, looking ever so calm, cool and collected. And utterly handsome. Unbidden, warmth flooded her belly, and that infuriated her. She couldn't be attracted to him.

Add to that, had she really stooped to questioning a

guest? "I'm sorry. I don't know what got into me, but I'm just a little freaked out."

He gently took her shoulders and guided her over to the big overstuffed sofa. "Sit here. Relax."

He joined her on the immense plush furniture.

"You have skills," she said. "I noticed that today. You had told me you were a security consultant. I had thought IT—information technology."

He huffed out a laugh to go with his grin. "I used to be with the United States Diplomatic Security Service."

Slowly she nodded, understanding so much more now. "Used to be?"

His brow furrowed and shadows darkened his blue irises. "I protected a diplomat on my last assignment. A foreign dignitary visiting the US." He paused as if considering his next words. "Now I'm a private security consultant."

Jonna sensed that a lot hung between those last two sentences. Ian held back.

"A private security consultant. What is that exactly? You mean a bodyguard or a private investigator?"

His features twisted up as he contemplated his reply. "Maybe a little of both, but it's less about muscles and guns. More about identifying potential danger and stopping it before it can happen."

"I see. That makes sense. I'm sure that's probably what you did with the DSS. Keeping diplomats secure is more about brains over brawn. Planning and preventing."

"Right. Preventing rather than countering an attack. But we're thoroughly trained to do both if necessary."

She didn't doubt that one bit after what she'd seen today. Regret poured from his eyes. What had happened?

He averted his gaze, staring into the flames. "I'm here

for obvious reasons—to watch the storms—and maybe a few not-so-obvious," he added.

When his gaze lifted to meet hers, she knew his words held a hidden meaning. What was it? His intense regard drew heat up her spine. Was she reading more into his words than she should? "I…uh…" Could she be more of an idiot? He hadn't been talking about her, as in he was here for her or for them. There was no *them*. What was it about Ian that had her thinking along those lines?

Oh, I'm in trouble. I'm in big, big trouble.

She buried her attraction. What was wrong with her? She didn't know the man. Didn't know whom she could trust. She didn't know if today she'd faced off with Washington's serial killer or…or…if her past had caught up with her.

Please, God, let it not be so!

He'd been perfectly fine with her making her own assumptions about what a security consultant would do. Except now Ian had said more than he'd wanted. Talking about his previous job this much brought on anguish.

Admiration flickered in her gaze before she shuttered it away. "Well, your previous job training certainly explains why you were able to take that guy down today. At least until the ocean interfered. So what happened? Why did you leave your job to become a private security consultant?"

Ian pushed up from the sofa to stoke the fire again, though it needed none of his attention. He tried to shut out the unsettling noise of the wind, with its eerie wail. Would this storm ever end? He might be concerned about the targets he and Jonna presented by sitting in front of the big panoramic windows, except he knew no one could survive on the beach at the moment.

He sensed her eyes on his back, just as he had sensed her watching him earlier. Despite her appreciation of what he'd done for her, she was wary of him, especially now. A little truth wouldn't hurt. She deserved that after all she'd been through. Although he hadn't wanted to have to share that particular truth.

"Ian," she said softly. "You don't have to tell me. I shouldn't have pried."

"No, it's okay." Was it? "It's not something I like to talk about. Something bad happened on my watch." *Somebody died.*

"And they fired you?"

Needles pricked over his skin. "No. They wanted to transfer me. I could have moved to a different department." Where he wouldn't be directly responsible for protecting someone.

Why was he telling Jonna this? It would only wipe clean the admiration he'd seen in her eyes moments ago. He shouldn't care about that. He couldn't help himself. He glanced over at her on the sofa, still watching him, then the fire suddenly intrigued her.

"But you didn't want to transfer?"

"No."

"You don't have to explain why. I can see in your eyes that you hold yourself responsible for what happened. I understand about that—" her downturned expression spoke volumes "—but you shouldn't blame yourself."

"How can you understand?"

"I guess that *understand* was the wrong word. Maybe I can't truly understand what you've experienced, and—"

She cut herself off abruptly. "Listen to me. I sound like a therapist."

If he could get her talking more about her background, he could potentially ease into the topic of the Miami criminals who might be after her. He wanted her to bring up the topic herself. If he broached it, he'd have to admit the real reason he was here, and he couldn't see that going well. From what Uncle Gil had said, and also from what he knew about Jonna, she would be furious about the fact Uncle Gil had hired Ian for protection detail. Maybe even shocked her old boss would hire Ian, of all people. Ian had been surprised himself.

Regardless, he couldn't risk her barring him from the Oceanview Lodge. Yes, in the worst case, he could watch over her from a distance. Still, that would be more difficult.

Ian put the poker where it belonged, but he remained near the fire. Jonna intrigued him in ways she shouldn't. He didn't want to be intrigued. However, he did want to come completely clean about why he was here. If Uncle Gil would just call him back, maybe the man would have some advice on how Ian could tell Jonna the truth without setting off her temper. But Uncle Gil hadn't responded to his voicemail. He should have heard back by now. That disturbed him.

She rose and joined him by the fire. So much for keeping his distance. She didn't ask more questions, seeming content enough with his answers. She had her own secrets, and he had his. But given today's events, it wasn't a good idea to keep his reasons for being here to himself much longer.

Come on, Uncle Gil. Call me back. Email me. Text me. Something...

The only person who'd tried to reach him today was Patrick, a good friend from his previous job, still working for the DSS. Patrick called every week or so, just to check up on Ian. He'd keep trying until he heard from Ian. But he didn't have time to call him back just yet. He was in the thick of this now.

The thing was, he couldn't be sure that the man who had shown up had anything to do with the women who were abducted, or if he had to do with the danger to Jonna from Miami. He would stick even closer and be more vigilant if she'd let him.

Tendrils of dread slithered over him as the anguish from his past assignment as a DSS agent filled his thoughts. His biggest failure had cost someone's life. Turned his upside down.

He couldn't fail again.

Jonna's life could depend on him.

Uncle Gil, what have you gotten me into?

FOUR

Back in her room, Jonna grabbed Chop Suey to snuggle beneath her comforter. The beast of a cat squirmed out of the covers and found a spot on the bed—his choice. When she'd first gotten him as a kitten, he'd jumped into her plate of Chop Suey, hence the name.

"It always has to be your idea, doesn't it?" She tucked the comforter under her chin. "Suit yourself."

For the first time she could remember, Jonna wished for a storm to end. The unceasing cacophony of crashing waves only stirred up the images from today like a reel-by-reel play. Vivid cinematography played across her mind.

A man pointed a gun at her, intending to kill her.

Add to that, that scenario had happened twice in her life. She wanted to know who that man was on the beach today.

She tossed and turned for what felt like hours. She even kept the cat awake. Eventually, Chop Suey jumped off the bed and found somewhere else to sleep. When Jonna woke up, it surprised her that she'd finally fallen asleep, but something had woken her.

What was it?

She remained still and listened.

It was quieter outside now.

The wailing gusts had moved on to torment another innkeeper up the coast. Another storm would replace it within the next few hours. Still, even now, sporadic gusts buffeted the cabin. The door creaked.

Probably nothing. Chop Suey didn't stir.

If she had known she would have to worry about the past, she might have gotten a dog. As it was, if she tried that now then Chop Suey would probably chase away any canine Jonna brought home.

Jonna grabbed her trusty Sig. She crept to the door and peeked through the peephole. She had a front entrance that didn't connect to the lodge to give her more privacy in case she ever went on, say, a date. Right. Through the hole, she saw nothing but darkness. She switched on the porch light. No one suspicious lurked near the door. She flipped the light back off.

Another creak.

This had to be the logs of the cabin shifting, but Jonna would take no chances after today.

Scritch, scritch, scritch.

The window this time. She rolled her shoulders and approached the window that faced the ocean. Now she wished she had closed the mini blinds and curtains.

Standing against the wall, she peered out and gasped, nearly screaming. She stepped back and pressed herself against the wall. She'd seen a shadow, the silhouette of a man. Hadn't she? Heart palpitating, she lifted her weapon and peered out again.

A tree branch morphed into the shape she thought she saw, then scratched the window. She was becoming entirely too paranoid. She couldn't function if she couldn't get any sleep.

In the meantime, she shut the mini blinds and tugged the curtains closed. Set the Sig aside and rubbed her arms. Pulling on a hoodie, she sat at her desk. It was much too late to call her old boss Gil, and besides, she dreaded that call with everything in her. But she had to find out if there had been more chatter.

What specifically had the chatter been when her name had come up? So she opened up her laptop, found his old email address—the one she hadn't used in three years— and typed up her question.

But she didn't send it.

This couldn't be about Florida. The guy thought he'd killed her—just a cop snooping around in a warehouse. She hadn't been targeted specifically.

Or had she?

She didn't know anything that would make her, personally, a target. There was no reason for anyone to think about her, much less say her name.

Jonna folded her arms on the desk and pressed her head into them. She was lying to herself. She tried to forget what she knew, which was very little. She suspected that not everyone involved in the human-trafficking ring had been taken down.

The mayor had wanted the case closed quickly. So the powers that be had conducted the raids and arrested the people involved. But not everyone had been caught in the net. Jonna had suspected someone higher up had been pulling the strings and had managed to avoid capture.

She was looking into that when someone had shot her and left her for dead.

Why would someone want to target her again? If they

did, that would only bring attention to the earlier attempt to murder her and the motive behind it. No, this simply couldn't be about Miami. She willed it to be so. Another lie. When had her will had anything to do with it? Jonna sent the email to Gil. She could trust him to be honest with her. He'd been good to her. Let her slip into obscurity quietly, the way she wanted.

If she learned one thing from today—it was that she was out of practice. At least she'd been jogging every day, but she was getting rusty to let that man pacing her get the upper hand.

She probably needed to hit the shooting range again, a place she'd avoided for much too long. She'd been foolish to think she could just walk away, start a new life. But it had been so very tempting, and Jonna hadn't wanted to work in law enforcement anymore. She wanted to live a peaceful life running a lodge on the Washington coast, and thanks to her aunt Debby's help, she'd been able to do just that.

Jonna had grown up in Coldwater Bay. Her aunt had raised her and her three siblings after their parents had been killed in a tragic accident. She'd been restless after her parents had passed away. They had been good people who were making a difference in the world when they'd died.

Jonna couldn't make sense of their deaths or her own life—what she should do with it. Aunt Debby had been the one to encourage Jonna when she said she needed a complete change of scenery. So Jonna went off to school in Miami. Maybe she'd ended up on another coast, but it was a coast at the opposite end of the country with completely different scenery and culture.

There she'd attended the police academy, following

in her mother's footsteps in law enforcement. She ended up working for ICE. It was brutal work—the horrors of humanity came to light every day—but she was proud that she made a difference in the lives of others.

At least that's what she'd told herself. Hadn't her parents been about making a difference? They would have wanted no less for her.

But in the end, she'd run from it all. Now she was glad to be back and closer to her siblings. Sadie, a marine biologist, and Cora, an underwater archaeologist, had taken the road of science after their father's example, and Quinn went into law enforcement like Jonna and their mother. He was a DEA agent. Unfortunately, she hadn't seen Quinn in years. He was on a deep undercover assignment—he'd dropped off the face of the earth. She hoped he was okay. She knew from personal experience just how dark the criminal world could be.

Drowsiness finally claimed her with only maybe a half an hour before twilight. But Jonna would grab what sleep she could. She slipped back into bed and Chop Suey joined her this time, snuggling up against her back. *I feel loved.*

She smiled, but with the thought of love came the sudden sense of loss, of what she was missing. Sadness pricked her heart. Of course Ian's pensive blue gaze, strong jaw and diplomatic security service skills had to fill her thoughts.

Now she would never get that sleep.

Ian had learned long ago through rigorous training how to survive on little sleep. Good thing. After the intense conversation with Jonna, his mind wouldn't shut off. And when the storm died down—just a reprieve before the next storm bore down on them—he knew what he could do to put his time to the best use.

He'd donned dark clothing and climbed out the window. Jonna had a night clerk at the desk in case the guests needed anything, but the door remained locked after certain hours. He didn't want to raise suspicions or alarm by leaving that way. He slipped out the window, careful to remain near the lodge so he wouldn't stumble too near the cliff's edge.

What a perfect place to watch the winter storms. Icy cold bit his cheeks. He couldn't stay here long. But he might as well walk the perimeter. Ramp up his task of watching over Jonna.

Now, if only Uncle Gil would call him back. Maybe the man was in the middle of a serious investigation and hadn't had the chance. But still, it wasn't like him not to check in.

Clouds rushed quickly across the sky, and silver moonlight broke through, making the whitecaps look almost fluorescent.

Wow.

He could watch that forever.

But he was on a mission. Ian tugged out his weapon, prepared to use it. His footfalls couldn't be heard over the waves or the gusts of wintry wind. If he couldn't be heard, neither could Jonna's attacker should he try to approach at night.

Would the man return? He'd asked the sheriff's department if they could put a deputy on watch at the lodge, just to keep Jonna and her guests safe until the threat had been neutralized. But they were already pressed for personnel and couldn't spare anyone.

After he'd walked the length of the lodge and around

the front—the part facing away from the ocean—he spotted Jonna's cabin. Though connected to the lodge, it stood off on its own. An easy target for someone who knew where to look.

Ian waited in the shadows of the woods and let his gaze search the area beyond the parking lot. A copse of trees stood between the lodge and the road, thick on that side of the building. Someone could get close to her that way if not through these woods on the south side. He didn't like it. Ian gave a wide berth as he walked around her cabin, hoping, praying to God he wouldn't find anyone.

Or if someone truly had come to go after her again, that God would help him stop them. He wondered if it would feel like redemption, to succeed in this case. But success, saving Jonna, wouldn't bring Serena back.

His soul cracked a little. He couldn't let the past distract him if he wanted to protect Jonna.

God, help me. Help me forgive myself.

Steeling himself against the onslaught of anxiety, Ian closed in on her cabin, then hesitated. A nuance, a sensation, prickled over his skin.

Someone else was here.

He waited in the shadows of a large evergreen, the branches and needles scratching the cabin window with each gust of an angry ocean breeze. Sea spray blew over his skin, even from this height.

And still he waited.

That sensation was unmistakable. He'd learned to listen to it and it had never failed him.

Fifteen yards out, another dark figure in the night also wearing black moved catlike toward the cabin.

Jonna's cabin.

His breath came hot and fast, but Ian steadied it, reminding himself to stay focused and calm. He had to end this tonight. As the figure crept toward the cabin, keeping to the shadows, Ian waited for the right moment. No longer a DSS agent, he couldn't officially arrest anyone, but any citizen could stop someone from committing a crime and hold them for the authorities.

The creeper approached and positioned himself in front of the door. He was hunched over, his back to Ian, who could only assume the man intended to pick the locks.

Jonna was in danger.

Ian acted on instinct and, remaining in stealth mode, rushed forward, then snuck up behind him. His thick, black coat and hood left no exposed area. Not that that mattered. Ian didn't have to see skin to know where to thrust his weapon.

He lifted the Glock and jabbed the muzzle into the base of the man's skull. The perpetrator instantly stiffened.

"Hold it right there." Ian forced the threatening words out through gritted teeth, remembering earlier in the day when someone had tried to kill Jonna. Was this that man?

Ian's nerve-endings prickled, aware the trespasser prepared to make a move.

"Don't even think about it. I'll put a bullet in your brain before you can move." Ian stepped a few feet back, putting space between him and his target so the man couldn't go on the offensive with a head butt or a kick. "Now, slowly back away from the door."

Suddenly it swung open.

Jonna!

Ian couldn't fire his weapon or he'd risk shooting

Jonna. The criminal ducked into the shadows, leaving Ian standing with Jonna pointing her weapon at him. Hadn't she seen the intruder at the door?

"Put your weapon down or I swear I'll shoot you." Her voice sounded every bit as threatening as his had sounded moments ago.

"Jonna. It's me. Don't shoot me, please. I'm lowering my weapon. In the meantime, the guy I found breaking into your cabin is getting away." Ian slowly lowered his weapon. She could have killed him.

"Ian?"

"Yes, it's me. Didn't you see him? He was picking your lock, Jonna. He slipped into the shadows when you opened the door. I'm sorry but I have to go after him. Stay inside and lock your door!" Ian backed away and then sprinted after the invader.

He feared he was too late, except for the footfalls pounding the ground resounded along the parking lot and indicated the man headed across the street.

Ian gave chase.

Behind him, Jonna shouted. "Ian, come back!"

Ignoring her, he headed across the street. A bullet whizzed by him. Uh-oh. From the dark forest, the criminal had the advantage now. Ian ducked behind a car. Jonna ran toward him as if she would crouch next to him. "Ian!"

But she wouldn't make it.

"Jonna, get down!" Ian dashed toward her and shoved her to the ground. A bullet grazed over his back, shredding his coat. He covered her body with his—an instinctive reaction. He hoped she understood. "It's not safe. Whoever this guy is, he fired a couple of shots using a silencer. You didn't hear them?"

"Not over the surf, no." Her breaths still came fast—she was like a frightened bird beneath him. She could definitely handle herself, but someone had targeted her tonight. Again. That was enough to rattle anyone. Ian's protectiveness kicked in, and this had nothing at all to do with the job his uncle had hired him to do. He felt personally compelled to keep her safe.

You can do this, Ian. You've got the skills. I trust you to protect someone special to me. Uncle Gil's vote of confidence rang in his ears now. Ian realized this assignment might have had something to do with building Ian's confidence again to begin with, but today, everything had changed.

Jonna's life was in danger. Ian was back in the line of fire. Would he be enough to protect her?

"You can get off me now, Ian."

"What?" He peered down into her gorgeous eyes and stunning features. Not what he needed to be thinking about.

"I'm safe now. You can stop covering me."

He shook off the daze. "Right. But let's stay down in case he hasn't gone."

"I don't want him to get away." She tried to free herself from Ian's protective cover. "Let's go after him."

Ian refused to release her. Not yet. "I'm not getting up unless you promise me you're not going to follow him. It's dark and dangerous. It's too risky. Our only option now is to call the sheriff again and tell him the guy returned for you." Looked like she was a deliberate target after all, and not necessarily a random victim on the beach earlier. He wasn't sure which was worse.

"What? You want me to have the sheriff come out here

and wake my guests? They're not in trouble. I am. Besides, the sheriff won't be looking for him tonight either."

"Promise me."

Jonna jabbed him in the solar plexus and pushed him off. Ian groaned. He grabbed her arm. "You're not going to chase him."

She stiffly nodded her agreement and he slowly removed himself from protecting her. "You shouldn't stay in your cabin tonight. It's too exposed. Move into one of your guest rooms."

"I'm booked."

"You can take my room. I'll stay in the cabin."

She shook her head. "I won't put you at risk."

"We'll figure it out tomorrow. Just for tonight, I'll sleep on the couch in my suite."

Jonna hung her head. "I can't believe this is happening."

"We can talk about it inside," Ian said. "Let's get you out of harm's way."

"I'm sure the guy is long gone by now." She crouched behind a vehicle as if uncertain of her words.

"We can't be sure." He peered into the woods.

"We can be sure of one thing," she said. "He wants to kill me."

Unfortunately, he agreed. He wanted to go search for the man and end this, but Jonna would insist on coming too. He wouldn't be in a good position to protect her if that were the case. "How about it, then? I'll watch your back tonight and sleep on the sofa."

"I don't know what to say."

"How about *yes*?" Still wary of the dark woods across the street, Ian climbed to his feet, weapon at the ready. "Besides, it's almost morning."

After the day they'd had, Ian suspected that daylight wouldn't chase the bad guys away, and Jonna would remain in danger.

FIVE

The next morning, Jonna rolled out of the guest bed and snatched Chop Suey to her. The twenty-pound cat had spent most of the evening on the prowl, exploring this new-to-him room with new smells and new corners and hiding spots to investigate. Jonna could only be glad her cat hadn't found any vermin. Already eight—she'd slept far too late, and hoped DiAnn had taken up the slack.

Cracking the bedroom door, she spotted Ian sitting on the sofa. True to his word, he was keeping watch.

Was he awake? No. Eyes closed, he must have allowed himself to finally sleep—albeit sitting up—since guests were awake and moving and no one would be so bold as to attack her in the lodge in broad daylight. On a deserted stormy beach, yes. In her lonely cabin at night, yes. But not now. She instinctively knew that Ian wasn't the kind of man who would have slept while he watched over her if he thought there was any chance she was in imminent danger.

That gave her a measure of relief.

For a few seconds, she allowed herself to freely take in his sturdy form and good looks. She admired his angular, scruffy jaw. Thick, dark hair that shagged a little around his ears and collar. His broad shoulders and demeanor that said he was ready to pounce, asleep or not, because his hand was pressed over his gun.

He had a gun.

That was a fact she should have been quicker to take note of last night. The exhausting day and her lack of sleep had left her too drained to acknowledge he'd been armed.

But she acknowledged it now.

Hmm.

She was definitely getting rusty. Holding Chop Suey, she crept toward the door. The last thing she wanted was to wake Ian. He needed sleep. Maybe she should wake him up just to let him know he could have his bed back. *Nah.* Jonna wanted to go back to her cabin and her privacy without Ian trying to stop her. She had a feeling he wouldn't want to let her out of his sight once he was awake.

More than that, she wanted to put distance between her and this over-the-top guy. He was a protector, all right. It was so easy to picture him in his position at the DSS. She didn't understand how he could have left such a promising career behind. Last night, he'd been her hero. She simply couldn't reconcile the bits of what he'd told her with what she knew of him.

Quietly she crept to her exit, shushing Chop Suey, who wanted down. She gently opened and shut the door, then snuck down to her own cabin entrance.

She reached for her own weapon that she'd tucked away in her hoodie and held it at the ready while holding Chop Suey in the other hand.

Adding in she had to unlock the door, this wasn't the best strategy.

Chop Suey escaped and ran the other direction right as the door opened. She should focus her attention on clearing her cabin to make sure it was still secure, but she couldn't let that cat encounter any guests. Chop Suey was huge and not all that friendly. Jonna shut the door and turned to catch her cat.

Ian stood there, holding the beast, who didn't resist. *Really.*

"What are you doing?" he arched a brow.

"I'm going back to my cabin to get dressed. I'm late for my job. In case you didn't know, I run this lodge."

"Why didn't you wake me?"

"I thought you needed the sleep."

"For your information, I wasn't asleep when you snuck out. I just wanted to see if you would wake me."

Of all the...

Though a half grin hitched up his cheek, his eyes remained dark as he handed over Chop Suey. "I'll check your cabin for you, just to be safe."

He pushed by her and with his weapon he cleared her small cabin. She followed him inside and released Chop Suey to run free. When Ian put away his weapon, he studied her.

"Listen, I appreciate what you did last night," she said. "You have skills and they came in handy. You keep saving my life. But you don't need to always be jumping in. I don't need protection."

He crossed his arms, unconvinced.

"There's something I need to tell you," she said. "Something you don't know about me."

"There's a lot I don't know about you, Jonna." The way he said the words, the look in his eyes, said he wanted to know more, and for far different reasons than simply to protect her.

"Before running the Oceanview Lodge, I worked for ICE as an agent in the Homeland Security Investigations division."

At her words, an emotion she couldn't read flashed in his gaze. "So you think that means you don't need help against a man who wants to kill you?"

"I…" Is that what she'd meant? "I just thought you should know that I'm not a helpless damsel in distress."

"Your actions on the beach, searching for the guy afterward and then again last night told me that you had a law-enforcement background."

Good. He understood. And since he knew she wasn't helpless, he'd leave her cabin now, right? Facing off with him, she crossed her arms. She could be equally as determined.

"Do you want me to call the sheriff about last night or do you want to do it?" he asked.

"I think I'd like to go in to see him. There's no need to upset the guests by having him come here two days in a row. And it's not like he needs to come by to gather evidence. Any evidence that we might have found will be gone by now after the storm blew through." She opened the curtains and then the mini blinds to peer out at her amazing view. She loved it here. Why did some crazed man bent on killing her have to ruin it?

It was so quiet in the room, she might have forgotten Ian had remained in the cabin, but she sensed his nearness right behind her.

"How about we meet in an hour? I'll drive you in to see him. He'll want to hear the story from both of us. We could look at more mug shots too. See if we can nail the guy from the beach, who is probably the same guy as last night."

She nodded. "An hour, then."

She heard him walk away. The door opened and shut. She had the feeling that he wouldn't be too far from her. It was as if he'd taken her on as his personal protection project. Jonna rubbed her arms. The idea sent tingles over her, which was the most inappropriate response. She wasn't at all sure how she felt about that.

Chop Suey mewled as if missing the guy already. Then he hopped on his favorite chair, ignoring Jonna completely. "So you prefer Ian, do you?"

Her cat hadn't liked anyone except Jonna. Ever.

Traitor...

She ran her fingers through the furry softness, sending shedding hairs drifting through the air.

She wouldn't think about how Ian made her feel or the attempts on her life. Instead, she'd think about something easier to handle—how furious she was that this had disrupted her morning jogging routine.

His breath puffed out in white clouds as Ian leaned against his silver SUV, waiting for his cell to connect.

Come on, come on, come on. Pick up the phone, Uncle Gil.

If only his uncle were still married then he could call his aunt and find out about what Uncle Gil was up to—and if the man was all right. But Uncle Gil and Aunt Sarah divorced years ago, and calling her to ask about Gil's whereabouts wouldn't accomplish anything except to upset Aunt Sarah. Nor could he call his mom. She would worry about her brother, maybe unnecessarily. Plus, she'd ask too many questions about what Ian was up to.

He released a heavy sigh, his concern for his uncle weighing on him.

The call went straight to voicemail. Again. He was probably driving his uncle crazy. But the guy needed to know about what was going on here in Washington. Ian would also like to know if there was any more intel there in Miami—something definitive regarding those Gil thought had an interest in Jonna.

But Uncle Gil had been her boss at the time. Those with a grudge against Jonna might also have a grudge against him. Was he ignoring his calls because he was also under attack? Ian didn't like having to worry about two people at once. But he knew where his attention needed to stay. Uncle Gil had hired him to shadow Jonna and protect her if needed. He must have thought the threat could possibly materialize, or why else send Ian?

Jonna was his priority, so he let his concern for his uncle go for the moment and considered the facts. Last night had been another close call. It had definitely been directed at Jonna.

Still, that didn't mean this guy wasn't the Shoreline Killer. He could be angry because he failed and have targeted her for that reason alone.

He jammed the phone in his pocket and paced as he waited for her. He made a futile attempt to shove away his fear—why was this happening? Why did he have to care this way about someone who was in danger? He couldn't go down this road again.

An icy gust hit his cheeks like pinpricks. The biting, cold morning was the slap in the face Ian needed—a good dose of reality. He couldn't let himself be drawn to Jonna—a woman he was protecting. As if conjured by his thoughts, she stepped out of the front of the lodge wearing a black leather formfitting jacket—*nice*—and hurried over to where he waited, carrying a paper sack and a drink tray holding two cups.

"I've been looking for you. Lisa told me you were out here. Why don't we take my vehicle?" she asked.

"Because mine is already warming up." He walked with her around to the passenger side of the SUV, taking in the savory smell of hot coffee and something sweet, then opened the door for her. "What have you got there?"

"Coffee and blueberry scones. That all right with you?"

"Always. Thanks for being so thoughtful." He held the snacks while she climbed into the vehicle.

Retrieving the cup holder and sack, she gave him a funny look. "I still think we could have just taken mine."

He got it. She didn't like relinquishing control over her life, even if it meant someone else was driving. She didn't know Ian all that well either, so trusting him to be in charge was a challenge.

He waited to reply until after he had gotten into the driver's seat.

Ian buckled and looked her way. "Humor me, will you? Someone tried to kill you twice. Taking mine will switch things up." Although on the one hand, drawing the man out if he chose to follow her might not be such a bad idea. But that wasn't their mission today.

"Suit yourself," she said. "I just don't want to be a burden to you."

Is that the reason why she wanted to take her vehicle? *Burden me, please...*

He grabbed the warm cup and sipped the coffee to test the temperature. Boiling hot. Just what he needed to take the edge off his chilled extremities.

If only she knew just how much he didn't mind helping her. "Thanks again for the coffee."

After steering out of the parking lot, he drove while he ate the scone, grateful she'd thought of food.

"How's the scone?"

"I can't complain." He grinned.

"What? You don't like it?"

Her reaction reminded him of his mother's when he didn't offer adequate praise for something she'd cooked. Admittedly he'd downplayed his enjoyment because he had wanted to see what Jonna would say.

"It's delicious. I've eaten these before at the lodge. Do you make them?"

"I wish. DiAnn bakes those up fresh in the kitchen every day. I wanted the lodge to have the feel of a bed-and-breakfast with homemade goodies in the morning. But sometimes we get breakfast from the restaurant next door. I'm glad we have that option."

"I envy you. It's a nice setup. Tell me, how does an ICE agent from Miami end up serving coffee and scones for breakfast in Coldwater Bay—an obscure part of the Washington coast?" He hoped he hadn't stepped over the line, bringing up her past.

Until yesterday, they'd kept a comfortable distance between them—a loose rapport that didn't require giving up secrets or sharing anything too personal—but that gap of mutual aloofness was beginning to narrow, and it had started with the attack on her life. Would she see it the same way?

"Do you mind if we don't talk about that?"

Guess not.

He'd opened up last night more than he'd wanted, sharing about *his* past. Ian worked his jaw. He didn't want to get on Jonna's nerves. They were stuck in this vehicle together for the forty-five-minute drive, then at the sheriff's department for who knew how long.

"Listen, I'm sorry," she said. "I didn't mean to snap. I know you shared with me about how you ended up as a security consultant now. I shouldn't have pried like that, especially when I know what it's like to not want to talk about the past."

And here, Ian had decided he was glad he'd shared with her. "It's all right, Jonna. If you don't want to tell me, you won't hurt my feelings. I'm a big boy."

"It's not that I don't want to tell you, but more that I'm not ready to talk about it with anyone."

Ian understood. Jonna was still processing the recent events and considering what any of it had to do with her job back in Miami.

Forty-five minutes later, Ian steered the SUV into the parking lot of the county sheriff's department. Sheriff Garrison had assured them he would be waiting. A deputy ushered them back to the sheriff's office where he spoke with a couple of deputies before they headed out. Sheriff Garrison welcomed them and gestured for them to sit. He took a seat behind his massive, paper-covered desk. When did he have time to go through all that?

"So you're here to file a report about what happened last night. Another attack?"

Ian and Jonna started speaking simultaneously, then stopped. Ian gestured to Jonna. "Go ahead."

"I kept hearing noises and couldn't sleep. I initially chalked it up to the cabin creaking, but then I heard something at the door. Even Chop Suey's ears perked up."

"I'm sorry." Garrison cocked a brow. "Chop Suey?"

"My cat."

Ian gestured with his hands. "An enormous cat. More like bobcat. Think a lion cub."

Jonna shot him an incredulous look. "He's a Maine Coon. They're big."

Garrison cleared his throat. "Let's get back to your story." He typed notes into his computer.

An investigative deputy would normally handle this and Ian appreciated the sheriff talking to them himself—like he'd done yesterday—rather than turning her over to one of his investigators. If this involved the Shoreline Killer, the sheriff wanted to be hands-on.

"I peered out the peephole and saw a man. More like two shadows, actually. I grabbed my weapon and opened the door."

"Hold on," the sheriff said. "You opened the door to face off with two perpetrators alone?"

"What was I supposed to do?"

"Call the deputy there in Windsurf."

"The man was picking my lock. He would have been inside in another minute and the deputy would have taken at least ten to get there. There wasn't time," she said. "You know that."

Garrison's face was unreadable. He didn't respond.

"Let's not forget you aimed your weapon at me," Ian said.

"Well, as soon as I opened the door, the guy ran off, and Ian was left standing there, but I didn't know it was him, see?"

"I had things under control." Ian wanted to watch the sheriff, but Jonna held a challenge in her voice that he had to respond to. He stared at her instead as he spoke. "I had my own weapon at his head and told him to back off.

You opened the door, a distraction, and he took off. I was left to stare down the barrel of your gun aimed at me."

"Well, how was I to know what you were doing? It's not as if you called me or texted me to read me in on what was happening."

"All right, boys and girls, just calm down. Did either of you get a good look at him?"

"He was dressed in black." Jonna eyed Ian, her thoughts clear.

So were you.

"So I take that as a no. Do you think it was the same guy who tried to shoot you on the beach?"

"Yes." Ian and Jonna said together.

Sheriff Garrison frowned and appeared to read through what he had so far. "Mr. Brady, why were you outside at that hour and why did you have a weapon?"

Good question. Ian resisted the urge to scratch his jaw. Might as well come clean. The sheriff had likely already looked into his background and simply wanted to hear confirmation from Ian. "I work as a security consultant. I was previously with the US Diplomatic Security Service."

"So you were a fed with the State Department. That still doesn't answer my question."

The look in Garrison's eyes told him what he already suspected—the man *had* looked into his background. Did he know what happened and why Ian had left?

Ian nodded. "I guess you could say I'm a protector by nature. When the storm died down, I couldn't sleep and thought I'd check the perimeter. After all, someone had attacked Jonna the day before. I'm glad I was out there because that's when I saw someone keeping to the shadows and making their way to her cabin. It looked as though they were trying to pick her locks. That's when I made my move, and you know the rest."

The sheriff gave Ian a nod of approval. "Jonna's fortunate you were there. Good work."

"Now, wait a minute," she said. "I'm perfectly capable of taking care of myself. I knew someone was trying to break in. Give me some credit, will you?"

"I know your background," Sheriff Garrison said. "But even law enforcement needs backup at times, Jonna, wouldn't you agree?"

Frowning, she shrugged. "I suppose so."

"He's more than qualified. More than capable. Maybe you need to hire Ian here as a bodyguard until this is over, unless he has another assignment. I don't have enough manpower to put a deputy on you full-time, though we could check with the state police if you'd prefer to take that route."

"No, thanks, I'm fine." Jonna peered at Ian as if begging for his help with the sheriff. "Really."

But he knew she would never hire him.

"I'm not going anywhere, Sheriff," he said. "I'll do my best to help." *And not just out of the goodness of my heart.* Though if Uncle Gil hadn't hired him, he might have found himself protecting her anyway because that was who he was—a protector at heart. He couldn't walk away from her now that he was sure she was definitely under threat.

"Now, how about you look through some more mug shots to see if we can find this guy."

Inwardly Ian groaned. It wasn't that he didn't want to find the man, but looking through so many photographs was too grueling, too time-consuming. He wished they could get a sketch artist involved, except they hadn't seen enough of his features.

He had a feeling Jonna groaned inside too, and not just because anyone would detest the task. No. It was because they had an inexplicable connection. She probably sensed that too.

His heart was on dangerous ground.

SIX

After browsing through too many mug shots, they finally headed back to Oceanview Lodge. Jonna stared out the window, feeling trapped by circumstances out of her control as Ian chauffeured her in his SUV. She didn't have time for this. This was her busy season, her favorite season. The best time to enjoy the storms. How dare some would-be killer interrupt her life. Frustration coursed through her veins, and admittedly, not just a little fear set her on edge.

"I owe you for bailing me out back there," she said.

"You don't owe me a thing."

"You got the sheriff off my back about extra protection. I don't need the state police hanging around. That would scare my patrons off."

"I meant what I said." Ian switched on his blinker to exit the highway onto the two-lane road. "I'm here, so you might as well use my skills as needed."

"But that's just it. I don't need your help, Ian."

"You don't *need* my help, or you don't *want* my help?"

She stifled a sigh. "I don't want to put you out. I'm not exactly in a position to hire a bodyguard."

"You don't know how much I charge."

"I have an idea. But the fact is that you saved my life twice. Now that I know that someone has targeted me, I'll be on alert."

"Remember what the sheriff said. Even law enforcement needs backup. I wish you wouldn't refuse my help. You're good at what you do and so am I. It's not like I can turn that off. I can't just stop protecting you, Jonna."

She slowly turned to stare at him. He kept his focus on the road, but he had to know she was studying him. His strong jaw, thick dark hair shagging down over his ears. She imagined what he would have looked like when he was a federal agent with the DSS—a crisp haircut for one, and that scruff on his jaw wouldn't be there.

Unfortunately, it made him all the more attractive to her. And his eyes…his eyes were the most intense shade of blue she'd ever seen. She'd sensed there was something special about him, and she'd had the utmost respect for him before she'd even known how much he deserved her respect.

"I have an idea." A dimple erupted in his cheek.

Oh yeah, and cute dimples too. He had those.

"I'm not sure I like the sound of that." She returned her focus to the road. Enough of looking at Ian.

"Chicken."

"So try me." She stifled her grin.

"There's a shooting range up the road. What say we go hone our skills? Both of us could probably use the practice."

She liked the way this guy thought. Hadn't she just been thinking she needed some training? They thought too much alike. "Hmm. You know what? That isn't a bad idea. Not bad at all."

"Will Chop Suey be okay if you don't rush right home?"

She chuckled. And a sense of humor. Definitely, he had a sense of humor.

"I mean, you did act like you answer to that beast."

"That's it." She gave him a friendly punch. "You'd better watch it, buster."

His laugh set something thrumming inside her. Something else to add to the things she liked about Ian. Okay now she was making a list. She absolutely could not make a list.

At the West Coast Shooting Range, Ian and Jonna paid a fee, then geared up to practice their shooting abilities.

He was good. Really good. Jonna had become rusty, but after several rounds, her technique returned. She should make it a habit to practice at a range, but she'd wanted to put the past behind her. This whole situation seemed surreal to her. Why now? Why had violence followed her here to Washington where she'd only wanted peace and to forget what had happened? She wouldn't find those answers here today, and since trouble had pursued her, she would have to be prepared.

She refocused on the task at hand and fired her weapon.

Through the Plexiglas that separated them, in her peripheral vision, she could see Ian's broad shoulders and muscular biceps, his steady aim. He hadn't seemed to lose any of his previous skills and likely had stayed in practice considering he was still "in the business."

Sensing he watched her, she lowered her weapon and pushed back her earmuffs when she noticed he had done the same.

"How about a little friendly competition?" he asked.

"You're on."

"New targets. Ten yards out. Whoever gets the most head shots wins." He arched a brow as he waited for her response.

"What's the prize?"

Warmth rushed to her toes with the look he gave her.

"I win, you have to go to dinner with me."

"And if I win, I don't have to go to dinner with you."

He frowned. Was that hurt in his eyes? She had to remedy that. "Wait. Let's have dinner either way. The loser buys."

"I don't think either of us will be losers, Jonna." That grin again.

Before Jonna secured her earmuffs back in place, she noticed a crowd gathered back against the wall and on the other side of the glass. The crowd couldn't know they were two former LEOs, but maybe their skills said enough. Ian watched and waited.

Jonna wished she would quit blushing when he looked at her. She shoved aside all those crazy feelings that Ian stirred in her and concentrated on her weapon—her Sig Sauer—and fired repeatedly at the target's head.

When it was over, Ian did the same.

Clapping resounded behind them. Jonna pulled the earmuffs off and they each retrieved their paper targets to compare. She shook her head. "I'm not sure which of us won."

Admiration shone in Ian's blue, blue eyes.

"Don't worry, Jonna. I don't mind buying dinner."

"Just as long as you know it's not a date." *It can't be a date.*

One thing she knew—it was becoming increasingly difficult to ignore her attraction to this man. Couldn't she just admire his good looks and obvious skills, his protective nature, without falling for him? Maybe she'd been lonely far too long.

She wasn't relationship material. If only she could confide in him about what she'd been through in Miami and not have to carry the burden alone. She shoved that unbidden thought away.

Ian ushered her out of the range. He gently touched her arm. "Are you all right?"

Oh, please don't do that. Don't touch my arm. Don't be all sensitive and caring. "Sure, thanks for this idea. The practice was good for me."

And now she had to have dinner with him.

One dinner that wasn't a date. Jonna wouldn't let herself be vulnerable enough for love, even for someone she somehow found herself connecting to, like Ian.

The afternoon had gotten away from them and dusk would be falling much too soon. Storm clouds pushed through and big droplets hit the windshield. They had passed the lull between storms, and Ian gripped the steering wheel, his focus on the curvy two-lane mountain road.

Sheets of rain made the path virtually impossible to see. He slowed the SUV, praying it wouldn't hydroplane right through the guardrail and off the mountain. He never thought those guardrails could stop a big vehicle on the move anyway.

"Maybe we should have headed straight back to the lodge," she said. "I wasn't thinking about the weather. The roads can get icy in the higher elevations too."

"We'll be fine." The words spoken for his benefit as well.

The rain eased up slightly and his shoulders relaxed. A glance in the rearview mirror made him tense again. It didn't matter they had taken his vehicle instead of hers.

"I think we're being followed."

"I noticed that too."

"When were you going to say something?"

"Just waiting on you to notice."

Had she noticed before him? They were much too competitive. But he didn't think she would keep that to herself if she had. No. The vehicle had been at the shooting range too, and before that in Bay City where they'd been to see the sheriff.

Had the driver been among those gathering to watch them shoot? Fury coiled in his gut. Anger at himself and his foolishness. He should have been more careful. Still, maybe their skills would warn the guy off.

If it was the Shoreline Killer.

"So what are you planning?"

"Let's see what he does. Right now, I'm focused on getting us back to the lodge." But he'd like to turn the tables on this guy.

The rain and wind picked up, pummeling the vehicle. The cab of the Suburban was warm and safe, but couldn't protect them against the cacophonous sounds of the storm. Rear lights flashed red in front of him as cars slowed to a crawl.

Ian spotted a bridge coming up and he steered onto the shoulder beneath the overpass a few feet behind another vehicle. He set the hazard lights to flash and watched in the rearview mirror.

"Oh, this is good. I can't wait to see what he does next," she said. "Do you think he'll pull up behind us?"

"If he does that, duck down in the seat and call the police. You're the target. I'll get out and face off with him. Maybe we can hold him for the law."

"In a perfect world."

He chuckled. He liked her dry sense of humor, and flicked his gaze to hers, then back to the mirror. No point in taking in those warm browns too long. Or her luscious, long dark hair. It didn't help that he wanted to run his fingers through it—a thought he fought off several times a day.

How had she gotten under his skin so quickly? He'd only known her for a couple of weeks, though he'd read the information Uncle Gil had provided and already knew she'd been a skilled ICE agent before. And yet, someone had taken her out. Maybe he'd instantly connected to her then, understanding what it felt like to leave a career behind. Then meeting her up close and in person—he'd been captivated by her.

"I haven't hired you, Ian. Remember, you don't need to protect me."

"And don't forget, Jonna, that I can't stop protecting. That's what I do. That's who I am." And that's what made his past failure excruciating.

In the corner of his eyes, he saw that she pursed her lips. He allowed himself a look and wished he hadn't. In her gaze he saw that she was most appreciative of his protection, whether she would readily admit that to him or not. Uncle Gil's words came to him again, encouraging him that he could do this job. That he had all the required skills.

"It's who you are."

The rain let up and the car in front pulled back onto the highway. A vehicle passed them—a red Chevy crossover. He tried to catch the license plate, but mud hid the information.

"It's him," she said.

Ian waited until the Chevy was twenty yards ahead and then pulled onto the road into light traffic. "The rain kept him from seeing that we'd stopped."

"Let's follow him." Jonna sat up taller in the seat.

"My thoughts exactly."

He shouldn't follow the man now, while Jonna, the woman at risk, was with him, but as she continued to insist, she wasn't incapable of protecting herself. And if they could follow him and nail him, then a bad guy would be off the streets and Jonna would be safer. That was a win-win.

Ian could go home and let her get back to her life. He could get back to his own life far from her.

In that perfect world she'd mentioned, Uncle Gil would call him back and tell him to share his true reason for being at her lodge. In that perfect world he could fly down to Miami and check on Uncle Gil himself because deep down, he had a bad feeling that something had gone terribly wrong.

If he didn't hear from the man tonight, he wasn't sure what to do. He understood Uncle Gil's specific instructions not to tell Jonna. She would boot him out of the lodge and warn him off, especially if she knew he'd been hired as her secret bodyguard.

The Chevy they followed recklessly swerved to the left to pass another vehicle. It was much too dangerous for Ian to follow. Then the car in front of them swerved and spun, hitting another car. He must have realized

Jonna and Ian were now behind him and didn't care who he hurt in his attempt to escape.

Ian slammed the brakes as the SUV skidded forward, heading straight for a collision, and prayed under his breath.

SEVEN

Jonna drew blood as she bit her lip. But she refused to scream as the SUV they were in lost traction on the slippery road and barreled toward the accident. This was exactly how people got killed.

Ian swerved and braked again, missing the two vehicles stopped in the road by mere millimeters. Jonna released her pent-up breath. "We have to get out and see if someone's hurt. Call emergency services."

"You call. *I'll* get out." His tone challenged her to argue.

But she wouldn't quarrel, and instead nodded agreement. There wasn't time to waste in getting help. Jonna called 9-1-1 and reported the wreck—the vehicles twisted together in the road. The detrimental weather reduced visibility and created a dangerous scenario for approaching traffic.

God, please help!

After the call, she got out of Ian's SUV and spotted him checking on passengers in the two cars that had collided. Even though his attention and concern was focused on others right now, she had the feeling he would know she'd gotten out of his SUV and into the storm, both literally and metaphorically.

The cold rain continued to pelt her and soak through her clothes. Shivering, she rushed up behind Ian to see what she could do to help as he leaned into a vehicle.

Though she stood behind him, he grabbed her hand without even looking. "Can you stay with her? She's unconscious. I think she bumped her head. I hope it's only a concussion. There's a child, a little girl, in the car seat in the back. She's okay, just upset."

Jonna nodded, offering comforting words to the crying child, but given the situation, they fell flat. She also remained aware of her surroundings, her previous law-enforcement background naturally kicking in. More than that, she kept her guard up for the man who wanted to kill her.

In her gut, she knew that *he* had caused this. The man who'd followed them. He was willing to risk others' lives for the chance to hurt her. Fury gutted her. A measure of guilt surfaced.

Someone wanted to hurt her and didn't care who got in his way—Jonna wasn't sure what else they could have done in this situation.

Emergency sirens resounded. In the distance, an ambulance raced past cars traveling along the shoulder. Troopers arrived in their state vehicles.

The woman whose hand Jonna held groaned and opened her eyes.

Jonna crouched next to her and squeezed her fingers. "Help is here. You're going to be all right."

Fear and confusion filled her eyes. "Kimmie?" the name croaked out of her mouth.

The child's eyes widened.

"She stopped crying when she heard your voice," she told the woman, trying to give her a comforting smile. Then she stepped back and a paramedic took Jonna's place.

Time to find Ian. She glanced over the hood of the car at the crowd and searched for him. He wasn't there. Then she turned and found him right next to her. Entirely too close.

Rain poured down his face, clung to his eyelashes, flattened his thick hair. Still, his blue eyes shone like a light in the storm—reminding her of a lighthouse that helped those in troubled waters navigate.

She wanted to lean in and cling to him.

He was right—once he decided to protect her, she wouldn't get rid of him easily, even if she wanted to. And that was just it—she inexplicably wanted Ian to be with her through this.

He grabbed her hand. Together they jogged to the SUV and climbed in. She wished she had a towel to dry her hair off or to protect his seats from her wet clothes.

He didn't seem to care about that and steered slowly around the cars.

"I spoke briefly to one of the Troopers about what happened. Gave him my card. He might call later if he needs our statements about what we saw," he said. "Keep watching, Jonna. He might be waiting for us up the road."

"I don't know why it matters. He has to already know where I live." *What am I going to do, God?*

"True enough," he said, and reached over to cover her hand with his. "Are you all right? Too cold? Should I stop at the coffee shop and get us something hot to drink?"

He removed his hand and cranked up the heat.

"No." She rubbed her shoulders, thinking of those innocent people. Everyone had survived the accident, but it could have been so much worse. "I just want to get back to the lodge." Though she wasn't sure why, since she would just have to remain vigilant there. What was going on? A chill that had nothing to do with getting soaked to the bone frosted over her.

He'll try again.

Jonna wanted to stay strong, but this whole thing wore on her. She'd left her law-enforcement career behind for a reason. After what she'd been through, she simply didn't want that life anymore. Besides, it was one thing to protect others, try to stop or capture killers, but it was entirely different when it was her own life that was in danger.

"I have an idea," he said.

She heard the smile in his voice. "Trying to cheer me up?"

"Did it work?"

Amazing that he could read her mood so easily. "Maybe. What's the idea? I hope it's not about dinner tonight."

"No. It's been a long exhausting day."

"So what, then?"

"We looked at mug shots, but so what? We need to find out everything we can about these women he's taken and maybe speak to someone about his profile."

"I know what you're trying to do. You want to find out if it's the Shoreline Killer who has come after me. You want to either confirm or eliminate him as a suspect. But this isn't your investigation, Ian."

When he parked at the lodge, she remained in the vehicle. Ian sat with her. Both were deep in thought.

"I'm not sure what to do next," she said.

He hung his head, his dark hair sliding forward, then the bluest eyes ever seemed to see right through her. She knew he was a protector by nature, but she thought maybe he cared about her or else she wouldn't see that kind of concern there. Mingled with that concern was another kind of fear, as if he was afraid of letting her down. Had he loved and lost someone before?

One of his dimples appeared, but just barely. "Maybe we could get out of town until he's caught and you're safe."

"Not a chance. I have a business to run." And if this was the Shoreline Killer, then he would just focus on another woman when he figured out he couldn't get to Jonna. The thought didn't give her the warm fuzzies.

She opened the door and climbed out, not at all ready to leave the cozy cab or Ian Brady, the security specialist who had made protecting her his pet project.

She hurried over to her cabin in the rain, Ian on her heels, and opened the door. Ian yanked her back and entered first with his weapon.

"Really, I can help with this."

Ian held her back. "He isn't after me, Jonna. Let me do this."

Reluctantly, she stood back and waited, but she held her weapon ready just in case. After he cleared the cabin, she flipped on the lights. She tried to hug Chop Suey to her, but the cat scrambled away, clearly mad at her for leaving him for so long. An entire roll of toilet paper had been destroyed.

"Ian, go to your room. Change into some dry clothes while I do the same. I think I'm safe. It's broad day—" she glanced at the window.

He cocked a dark brow. "You were saying?"

"Well, it was broad daylight an hour ago. Let's change. I'll meet you in the kitchen. I need to catch up with DiAnn and let my employees know I'm still alive. I can't be running off like this on a regular basis."

"Okay. I'll meet you in five minutes."

She pointed at her hair. "With this wet mop, I'm going to need at least fifteen."

His gaze swept over her hair and appreciation flitted across his features before he left, leaving Jonna to fight the warmth flooding her heart. She did not wish to have this kind of reaction to the guy. But that didn't seem to matter anymore. Ian Brady had shaken her, shifting what she thought she wanted.

She sagged, then gave in and plopped on the sofa. Chop Suey decided to return and mewled, rubbing back and forth at her ankles. "I am in so much trouble, and I don't mean just because there's a crazy man out there who wants me dead."

Ian flipped on the television to see if there had been any news about the wreck. He could search the images for their man if the guy had stayed behind to watch the scene. While he watched, he quickly changed out of the cold, wet clothes and towel dried his hair.

Then iced over.

A new woman had been found dead. The Shoreline Killer had struck again? Ian slowly dropped to the sofa to watch the news story. He looked at the GPS on his phone and entered in the location. Fifteen miles north of Jonna's lodge. An image of the woman appeared on the screen. Long dark hair and brown eyes. Like Jonna.

What did it mean, if anything?

Ian checked his phone. No calls or texts or emails from

Gil. The man had sent him up here to watch Jonna, then vanished. Though it was after regular business hours, law enforcement never quit. Ian called the SAC field office where Gil worked. He would ask about Gil's whereabouts. He didn't care who he talked to. He finally got Uncle Gil's assistant Nadine, working late.

"This is Ian Brady. Gil's nephew. I've been trying to reach him for a few days now, but he doesn't answer. Is everything all right? I mean, he's not in a hospital in a coma somewhere, is he?"

She laughed. "No, but close. He's at a conference training and expo meeting with some bigwigs. I'm sure he'll get back to you as soon as he can. And if I talk to him, I'll tell him you're trying to reach him."

"I think he knows, but thanks."

Ian stared at his phone and frowned. Maybe he hadn't been clear enough with his message that something had happened. Still, it didn't seem like Uncle Gil to ignore a message—much less the string of messages he'd left. How hard would it be to take a few seconds to respond to a text? He grabbed his weapon and kept his phone out, then waited in the hallway for Jonna. She'd wanted fifteen minutes.

He'd given her ten.

Ian knocked.

"Just a minute," she called.

Finally, she opened the door. She'd changed into dry clothes—jeans and an alpine sweater. Her long hair was still wet and she was finger combing the tangles. "I'm not ready yet."

"Did you see the news?"

She froze. "News? What news?"

He glanced down the hall, then back to her. "Can I come in so we can talk in private?"

She hesitated. What was that about? Then opened the door wider. "Sure."

Ian entered the quiet cabin and Chop Suey rushed over to him, twisting around his legs.

"I don't get it," she said. "He usually doesn't like people."

"I'd say he's a great judge of character."

She lifted the cat and held the beast as if to put a barrier between them. "What did you want to talk about? What's the news?"

"Why don't you sit down?"

Lines creased her features. She was growing inpatient. "I'm good."

Okay, then. "Another woman has been found. They suspect the Shoreline Killer has taken another victim."

Jonna paled. "What?"

"You heard me."

"When? Where?"

"I don't know when, but they found the body fifteen miles north of here." And she looked just like Jonna. Ian wouldn't tell her that part. Had the man acted out in frustration because he hadn't been able to take Jonna?

Zombielike, she moved to the sofa and eased into it, releasing the cat, who dashed out of sight. Jonna pressed her face into her hands and slid her fingers up into her hair. Ian resisted the urge to sit next to her. Hold her and tell her it was going to be all right. He had no business being that familiar with her, or making those kinds of promises.

God, help me protect her.

Finally, she looked up at him. "What do you think it means?"

"We need to know more. If we could find out from the ME the exact time of death, that could tell us when she was killed in relation to when we chased someone away from your cabin."

She held out her palm. "That still wouldn't tell us what we really need to know, which is who this man is. And why am I saying *we*?" She shoved from the sofa and shook her head, deep frown lines in her beautiful face.

"It could possibly rule out the Shoreline Killer as your attacker. And I thought *we* agreed that I would help protect you until this was over."

"I never actually agreed to anything."

So they were back to this again. Ian released a heavy sigh. No matter. He wouldn't waste his time arguing with her. If he couldn't get ahold of Uncle Gil tonight after he sent an urgent message, he would tell her his role here at the lodge, even without Gil's permission. Maybe she would take him seriously then. He believed she was taking her attacker seriously, but was she even considering that the danger could come from Miami rather than from the Shoreline Killer?

"I know you have a law-enforcement background," he said. "I know you can shoot with the best of them."

Her lips formed a beautiful, soft smile. "You mean I can shoot on par with you. You're one of the best of them."

Was she paying him a compliment? "If you're not willing to get out of here—go somewhere far away for now—what do you say I sleep on the sofa again tonight? Just until we get a handle on what's going on."

Her chin jutted up with that forceful, determined

look—the cop in her coming out. He'd seen more of that over the last twenty-four hours. She'd left that behind and tried to get in touch with her softer side here at her lodge. He got that. But now Jonna the cop was reemerging. Either way, he found Jonna one of the most desirable women he'd ever met. Now, if he could only resist her.

Get a grip, Ian. Shut it down.

"Well?" He arched a brow. By the set of her jaw and the look in her eyes, she would say no. That would mean a cold night for Ian as he watched over her from the outside of her cabin to make sure no one tried to break in. The doors to the lodge were locked after nine at night, so he didn't have to worry about a break-in from the inside.

"Let me think about it."

She was full of surprises. Unfortunately, Ian liked that.

He liked that very much. Another sigh beckoned to escape.

He couldn't let himself fall for Jonna if he wanted to protect her. He'd fallen for the daughter of the foreign dignitary he was protecting, and she had been killed on Ian's watch. Ian had died with her—on the inside.

Becoming emotionally involved was never a good idea. The worst kind of idea.

A potentially deadly idea.

EIGHT

"Go on, Ian. I'm okay to dry my hair alone." She needed to talk to her employees, but feared her shaky voice right now would worry them. She needed a minute to pull herself together. "If you wouldn't mind, I'd appreciate if you could find DiAnn, Lisa or Kelsey. Anyone who works for me. Tell them I'll be there in a few minutes to find out how things went today."

He appeared uncertain but nodded his agreement and left her alone. She went into her bathroom and pulled out the hairdryer. She only cared about her appearance for her guests' sake.

Right. And maybe a little bit for Ian's sake. How was she going to shake that off? Why did she care?

More important things were going on.

A woman had lost her life. Maybe last night. Maybe after that jerk hadn't gotten his hands on Jonna.

Furious tears burned at the back of her eyes. She hated this. She hated all of it.

Her knees shook. Her hands trembled and she dropped the dryer. She snatched it up, shut it off and put it back in its place.

She didn't want to crumble.

But she couldn't stop herself from crumbling.

She fled to her bed and dropped to her knees, pressing her face against the mattress. Nobody could ever see her like this—how weak she truly was.

Nobody but You, God. Where are You in this?

Another woman…dead…

Jonna allowed the tears to flow now. Getting it over with rather than holding it in was for the best. Especially with Ian inexplicably tuned into her every mood. Why couldn't she have met a guy like him before she'd been emotionally obliterated and unwilling to let anyone get close?

God, show me what to do. I know when I'm weak You are strong. Be strong for me. Show me the way. Please don't let this man kill anyone else.

Jonna sat back on her haunches. Snatched a tissue from the bedside table and wiped her nose and eyes. Ian would come looking for her if she didn't show up soon. He wasn't the kind of guy to smother a person, but he was someone who had failed before, and had somehow assigned himself to watch over Jonna. Some sort of personal challenge, maybe? The stakes were high for him too.

She started to climb to her feet, then noticed something under the bed. A shell? She picked it up and examined it. A tulip shell.

Now, how did you get here?

She opened the drawer in her nightstand where a small box held a few items she'd brought with her from Florida. A chill crawled over her. She slowly got to her feet and reached for her gun on the table. Whirling, she stood where she was and studied the closet. The door remained closed. Ian had cleared the cabin when they got back.

That would mean he'd looked in the closet. Hadn't he? And she trusted him, but clearly someone had been here while they'd been gone. She hadn't opened the closet door to get dry clothes but had simply grabbed them from the laundry basket.

Slowly, she crept closer. Holding her weapon up and ready to use, she whipped the door open.

Empty. No one remained lurking in the closet.

She released a sigh of relief and eyed the shelf above the hanging clothes. The boxes. They were out of place. Someone had been searching for something. But what? What could someone possibly think she had?

Was the shell a clue? Was it confirmation the man after her here in Washington was connected to what happened in Florida?

But what about the woman killed not far from the lodge—near proof that the Shoreline Killer had struck again?

Regardless, someone had been in her cabin while she was gone. And while she was gone, someone had followed her from the sheriff's office, and he couldn't have been in two places at once. But he could have gone through her stuff because he knew she would be gone for a while, careful that he didn't disturb anything so she wouldn't know—fat chance—and then headed straight to the sheriff's department. Ian had a tracker on his vehicle. That had to be it.

They'd been there long enough; he could have easily caught up with them there. Watched and waited, then followed them.

Had he wanted to run them off the road when the opportunity presented itself? Had that been his intent?

She grabbed a hoodie, tucked her weapon away so

her guests wouldn't know she was carrying, then left the cabin. Jonna calmed her nerves and tried to walk steadily down the hall. She greeted guests in the main room as she searched for the dark-haired scruffy-jawed man. He was one of a kind.

She found him in the kitchen.

His dimpled smile sent the fireflies dancing in her stomach.

"Just the woman I was talking about," he said with a wink. Way to really lay it on thick so her employees would focus on the flirty vibes rather than worrying about her being in danger.

"I was just telling Lisa here," he said, "that you wanted to find out how the day went. Lisa told me that DiAnn left to run an errand."

Jonna nodded, wanting to speak with Ian about someone being in her cabin, but she reminded herself she had a lodge to run. "Hey, Lisa. Sorry about today. I'm still working with the sheriff about how to track down the guy on the beach. So how did it go? Any issues?"

Lisa was in her late twenties. Her blond hair was pulled back, but curls escaped and framed her face. She smiled. "You've trained us well. We know what we're doing and can handle things for a day or more. I mean, how hard can it be?"

Had she insulted Lisa? Jonna hadn't meant to. She just wasn't good at relinquishing control of any kind. Jonna smiled to put Lisa at ease. "I'm glad to hear that. Of course, you can handle things without me."

Lisa chuckled. "Well, we always *need* you, Jonna. I don't mean it like that. The lodge wouldn't be the same without you, and I'm sure some guests would agree." She shot her gaze to Ian. "But no one had any issues. It's been an amazing day to watch storms. DiAnn brought in corn bread and a big pot of chili from the restaurant next door for lunch. I'm just glad I wasn't out in the storm. Ian was telling me there was a wreck and you guys were almost part of it."

"It was Ian's quick thinking that saved us. It looked like the others involved will be all right."

"Well I'm just glad you weren't hurt. I'm about to take over the front desk from Kelsey. Is there anything else you need?"

"No. You're good to go. And thanks, Lisa."

Lisa left them alone in the kitchen.

Ian watched Jonna. What was he thinking? It didn't matter. They had other issues. Big issues. Jonna grabbed Ian's arm and surprised even herself with her forceful-ness as she dragged him down the long hallway back to her cabin. She opened the door, urged him inside and shut it behind them.

"What's going on?"

"We have to check your SUV. In fact, we should check both our vehicles in case someone put a tracker on them." Jonna explained that someone had been through her things while they were gone then showed up at the sheriff's department to follow them.

"Show me your closet."

"That's not important—it's not like you know what it looked like before it was rummaged through. Let's look at our vehicles."

"Fine, but tell me, what could someone have wanted from your closet? What were they searching for? We need to tell the sheriff this information."

She knew what he was thinking now. "I know. It's

not something the Shoreline Killer would have any reason to do."

Grabbing flashlights, Ian and Jonna searched his vehicle and removed a GPS tracker. She placed it in an evidence bag. They found one on her vehicle as well.

Standing in her private closed garage, she hugged herself. "I want to know how someone is getting in and out."

"I noticed you have security cameras."

"Only in the main lodge."

"Let's look at that." Ian took off his jacket and handed it to her. "Here. You're cold."

"I'm fine. I've made a decision."

"Oh?"

"I don't need you to sleep on the sofa to watch over me."

"Jonna…"

"I'm going to be watching the lodge tonight. I'm going to stake it out. Want to join me?"

"I have to advise against that. It's not the best way to remain safe and protected. But I can't stop you, and I happen to know you'll do it without me, so you're on." He cocked a brow. "And it's going to be cold out there, unless you want to sit in one of our vehicles." Ian hesitated, then, "Jonna, I don't know if he's going to come back to the cabin."

"What makes you say that?"

"For one thing he's already gone through your stuff—and left a sign he was there. He knows you're aware of the break-in and will be watching for him to return. I think a better angle for us to investigate is what he might have been looking for. It would be best if you could think about past cases in Miami, let's say." His eyes flicked to hers. He knew something. She could sense it. What had he learned? Fury boiled under the surface. She didn't like that he'd been looking into her past. But she didn't want to argue about it right now, so she focused on the other part of what he'd said.

"So why won't he come back to my cabin tonight? He wants to kill me, remember?"

"But he's already lost the element of surprise."

"Maybe. I still think it's worth it to stake out my lodge and cabin. We can borrow Lisa's car and sit in that to keep warm. She's working as the night auditor. Of course, I'll have to explain what we're doing and why, so that isn't so good."

"I don't think that's necessary. He's not going to be looking at my SUV to see if we're sitting in it. I'll bring the coffee and scones this time."

"Well, there you have it. You're buying dinner tonight."

"That isn't dinner. Eating at a stakeout is never dinner." He stepped closer to her then. Too close. Chop Suey wound between his ankles and hers as though chaining them together. "Jonna, we're going to get him. Don't worry."

His tone was reassuring. Even though she was angry with him, she still needed that from him. With the intensity in his eyes, she wanted nothing more than to believe Ian was right. If only they could nab the man who attacked and tried to kill her on the beach and, in doing that, also take out the Shoreline Killer.

Too bad she couldn't bring herself to believe it was going to end well.

Dressed in dark clothes—black jeans, turtleneck, leather jacket and knit beanie—Ian shivered and waited in the shadows near the lodge entrance. A security lamp barely illuminated a small circle of light in the parking lot, but lights shone under the awning over the doors to the lobby, leaving his position hidden. In the shadows he could keep an eye out.

At least it wasn't raining at the moment, though the wind had seriously picked up. He and Jonna had decided to look at the security cameras tomorrow so they would have more time for staking out the cabin. Besides, the security footage would only show them the guests, and it was unlikely any of them were involved. The employees would have noticed any suspicious behavior and said something, especially after what had already happened on the beach to Jonna.

The man's access point had probably been the private entrance to her cabin, though they hadn't been able to detect any forced entry.

Last night, the man had shown up in the early morning hours before dawn, but they couldn't count on him keeping to that strategy, if he showed up at all. When Ian spotted Jonna through the window of the main entrance to the lodge, he shoved from the wall and met her as she came out.

He tugged her into the darkness next to him. "I scouted the area already."

"What? Without me? We're supposed to do this together, remember?"

"And we will, but first I needed to make sure we're good to go for the stakeout. I didn't see him, so we have a window of opportunity to get inside my SUV. I warmed it up and moved it over there with the other guest vehicles. It's darker and he won't so easily spot us if he's looking."

Ian stayed close as they moved in the shadows to his

vehicle, then crept silently over. Jonna moved to the passenger side's back door. Ian nodded and quietly unlocked it. They each climbed into seats directly behind the driver and front passenger seat.

"The windows are tinted," she said. "He won't see us in here."

He and Jonna thought alike. Agreed on most everything, except for keeping her away from danger.

"You've used this for surveillance before?" Jonna pulled off her knit cap and finger combed her long hair.

"Maybe." Ian frowned. With Jonna next to him for hours, this would be a tight space. Doubt edged his thoughts. "It might be better if we just wait inside your cabin for him to show up."

"Something about waiting in the cabin for a killer to come and get me just doesn't feel right. At least it's nice and warm in here. Maybe too warm. You're not going to fall asleep, are you?" she asked.

"No. But I'm worried about *you*."

"At least I didn't forget." She stared at him. "You were supposed to bring coffee and scones tonight."

"I didn't forget either. It was more that I think we should stay on alert and not get distracted with food. Warm scones in our stomachs and we'd get too comfortable and fall asleep. If he came, we'd miss him. In fact, we should stop talking now. We don't want to scare him off, or have him catch us by surprise." Admittedly, he really should have brought thermoses of coffee. They might need the caffeine to stay awake. That misstep disturbed him. Jonna was already becoming a dangerous distraction to him.

He lowered the windows slightly, but not too much, so they could listen to night sounds. On this side of the lodge, the crashing waves weren't so loud, so they had a better chance of hearing someone's approach if they were quiet and paid close attention.

"It's going to be a long night," Jonna whispered, her attention on the dark woods.

"Though I didn't bring the coffee and scones, I did bring these." He tugged night-vision goggles from his pack on the floorboard. "I only have one pair. So we'll take turns."

Jonna frowned.

"Don't worry, I know how to share." Everything but his life. Years ago, he'd dreamed of someone to share his life with, but after everything fell apart, he'd become a broken man inside. Best not to drag anyone else down or put himself in a position to get more shattered than he already was. Unfortunately, Jonna had brought all those long-forgotten dreams back to life. Somehow he had to put them aside. That dream wasn't for him, even with someone like Jonna.

But despite his best intentions, he was sure it wasn't going to be easy to sit in close quarters all night with Jonna while they waited and watched for the guy to try again. Ian did his best to focus on why they were there, and not his personal issues.

Would her would-be killer really be so stupid as to come back tonight? The criminal had put a tracker on their vehicles. What else had he done? He might even see them sitting here, in which case Jonna's safety was definitely compromised. The SUV's windows were tinted, but they weren't bulletproof.

"The only way to get to the cabin is through this parking lot or those woods," he whispered, and peered through the goggles.

"You don't think he would risk going around the front of the inn?"

"In the dark with that cliff? No."

"You're probably right. Someone might see him in the panoramic windows. Anyway, I thought you said we should stop talking."

Right. Talking could give them away. So they sat together with the windows cracked as they listened.

Ian wanted to do more than talk. He wanted to shake Jonna. He wanted to make her tell him everything that had happened in Miami to bring her here. The professional story and the personal story, even though he knew that was none of his business. It burned him she hadn't opened up to him about Miami yet. He'd been transparent with her when he'd shared about his job and the tragedy that had happened while on his watch.

In fact, if she'd wanted more details, he would have given those.

Maybe. Or maybe he was lying to himself. Still, she'd held her secrets close when he'd opened up. At least she'd told him she'd been an ICE agent in Miami. That had made him hope she was starting to trust him. But then tonight, when she'd shared someone had been searching for something in her cabin, he'd given her the opportunity to tell him about Florida when he mentioned Miami.

She hadn't.

"You seem distracted," she whispered.

Ya think? He glanced at her, then away. He didn't want her to see his frown or know that he was brooding. The close quarters with her didn't help. His senses were on high alert, hoping the man would show up tonight and that this time they would take him down. But other senses were on high alert too, and not for reasons of his choosing. Jonna's essence, her nearness, pressed in around him. When she leaned over her long hair fell forward. He wanted to weave his fingers through the soft tendrils.

Not professional thinking.

He cleared his throat.

It didn't help that he sensed Jonna was attracted to him as well. They…worked well together.

Ian shrugged off the unbidden thoughts—everything to do with Jonna.

Hours passed. *2:00 a.m….3:00 a.m….4:00 a.m….*

Both experienced in their chosen line of work— though in Jonna's case that career was well in her past— they remained awake and on alert, but lost in their own reflections, hoping for the best, preparing for the worst.

Ian donned the goggles again and searched the woods. He turned to look behind them through the crack in the glass and froze. He touched Jonna. Motioned for her to pay attention.

He's coming…

When the prowler crossed the parking lot, keeping to the shadows as much as possible, Ian removed the goggles. Too much light from the security lamp rendered them useless. A shadow crossed in front of the vehicle. Ian stiffened. Jonna sat up. The plan was to let him enter the cabin and trap him there. He wouldn't be able to escape through to the lodge because of the dead bolts and locks—they would pin him before he could reach them.

Jonna gripped her weapon.

Ian grabbed her arm and leaned in close. "Stay here. Let me go after him," he whispered. He could plead with her one last time.

In response she slowly and quietly opened the door.

Ian got out too. Together they crept around into the cover of the woods and watched the man edging his way to the front of the lodge, near the windows—exactly where they thought he would never go.

Jonna motioned silently for Ian to go around the other side of the lodge and block his path that way. *No. Not happening.* He grabbed her and shook his head. Motioned for her to go around the other side. He would come at the guy from the near side where he was likely to face off with him before Jonna. She didn't look happy, but she complied.

If anything Jonna was professional. A team player. Add in Uncle Gil's words of admiration, and Ian knew the Department of Homeland Security had lost a good investigator when she'd left.

But this wasn't the way he would have wanted any of it to play out. Given his preferences, Jonna would be safely away in another cabin and Ian would be protecting her, but she was proactive, preferring to take the offense rather than waiting for someone else to take out the bad guys.

He got that about her. He liked that about her too. But the next few minutes would be telling.

Wearing the night-vision goggles again, he readied his gun and crept stealthily around the cabin entrance. Preparing himself for the unexpected, but hoping he had the advantage of surprise.

No one was there. Ian's pulse ratcheted up.

The man couldn't have escaped. But he *could* have continued on around the corner of her cabin and be hiding in the space between the cabin and the lodge. Another structure—the add-on that connected the cabin to the lodge—would prevent his exiting that way, but he could use the spot to lie in wait for an ambush. If he was hiding there, that could mean he was onto them.

Jonna hadn't made it around the other side yet. They should be trapping the man between them.

Then he saw her edge around the corner. He didn't like this. She should be somewhere safe, or at least by his side. Where had their perpetrator gone, and what would he do next?

Waves crashed against the shore, preventing him from hearing anything else.

But he *sensed* someone all the same.

The hair on his neck stood on end.

He whirled around to face this new threat. Lightning coursed through his insides, incapacitating his ability to move. To react. To think. Then his body was shoved out into open air.

NINE

"No!" Jonna screamed. *No, no, no. Ian!*
Oh, God, no! Please, God, no...

She'd made out his form, whirling around as someone approached from behind. Sparks. She'd seen blue sparks—a Taser? Then he'd been shoved off the cliff.

A fist squeezed her heart and wouldn't let go. But she had to keep moving. She had to finish this. She fought the weakness in her trembling knees. Resisted the need to crumble to the ground. To rail at God. This had happened to Ian because of her. But she couldn't wallow in the pain and guilt. Not yet. So what if her heart ached so much the pain was physical?

She turned on her flashlight as she pointed her Sig.

How had the man gotten the best of Ian? How had he come around behind him? She crept forward along the edge.

She could see him standing there. Waiting for her? Was this a trap? She aimed her weapon and fired multiple times. He disappeared from sight, but had she shot him? Her gut told her no.

Waves crashed angrily against the rocks below, drawing her thoughts back to Ian. Images of his broken body accosted her. If she actually saw them instead of just picturing them in her head, they would fracture her. No. She had to hold it together and get this guy. Get justice for Ian. But she couldn't make it all the way across so close to the cliff's edge. It was much too dangerous, and she was much too angry—crushed, more like—to be as careful as she would need to be.

Jonna made her way back the other way. She would find this jerk. He wouldn't leave after taking down Ian. Jonna was the one he wanted.

Well come and get me!

"Come and get me!" She yelled out loud this time. The waves and wind would probably prevent anyone from hearing her, but she willed him to come after her and this time, she was prepared. She would take him down.

Furious tears blurred her vision, making the path more treacherous. She pushed them back, fighting to rein in her feelings. She'd been a cop once. She mustered all of her experience, all her skills to face off with this man. Ian—if he was still alive—would be furious if she let her emotions put her at risk.

Maybe…maybe she shouldn't confront the attacker, just for Ian's sake. No. That was fear and cowardice talking.

Wind battered her against the windows of the lodge as she moved. She could make out the dying embers in the huge fireplace of the common area, but no one was up at this hour of the morning. Perhaps even the gunfire hadn't woken them, but had been absorbed by the wind.

Before she reached the corner, she pressed her back against the wall. Fear and grief squeezed her lungs. She couldn't get enough air. She shut her eyes and sent up a silent prayer for help as she sucked in a breath. Readying her weapon, she whipped around the corner, hoping for a reason to shoot.

The light at the lodge's entrance was out. But the security lamp in the parking lot remained on, allowing her to see the silhouette of a man standing there. He took a step toward her. Then another step, and another.

Until he marched toward her.

"Stop! Or I'll shoot."

He didn't think she would?

Then something flashed in his eyes. Unintentional telegraphing, indicating that someone was behind her. Her heart dropped to her feet even as she whipped her gun around.

Another man stood far too close. She kicked the Taser out of his hand and started to aim her gun, but the man had a hundred pounds on her in muscle, and knocked the weapon away before she could act. He tried to punch her, but she ducked.

Run. You can't fight both of them!

Jonna elbowed the man in the nose. Kneed him in his crotch. And turned to face off with the other one.

He'd closed in on them and used the opening to punch her in the face.

Pain ignited. Flashes of light swam across her vision. Rough arms grabbed her and lifted her. A dazed confusion gripped her thoughts. She didn't fall into unconsciousness, but the men carrying her seemed to believe she'd blacked out.

She could use that to her advantage.

But she had to wait for the right moment. They reached the sand. Cold, salty ocean spray soaked them all. The brute who carried her tossed her body onto the wet beach.

Maybe they would leave her there so the ocean would simply wash her away, believing she would drown.

But no.

She was wrong.

The criminal moved toward her in such a way, with a leer on his face. Jonna fisted sand and shoved to her feet. She tossed the handful in his face and turned to run. The other attacker caught her and slammed her to the ground.

Jonna would die fighting.

She shoved to her feet and rammed into him, amazed that she managed to push the two-hundred-pound brute to the ground. He must have lost his footing in the sand.

Jonna was used to jogging on this beach and was in shape. Those were her only advantages. She took off running. Fire lit her whole body up. Muscles seized as she was attacked with the Taser. She fell face-first into the sand.

I'm going to die on this beach tonight.

No one would ever find her after the storm. Her body was rolled over.

The smaller one stood over her then. His eyes gazing down at her. And it all came back to her. The face. The images. Everything from Miami. She recognized those eyes.

She knew the man.

He'd left her for dead before. She was sure that he wouldn't make that mistake twice.

Charging through the wet sand with his only weapon—a length of driftwood—Ian slammed it into the back of one gunman's head. The would-be killer dropped to the ground. Seawater washed up and over him.

Another figure stood over Jonna, a gun in his hand. He aimed it at her face.

"Jonna!" Ian called. *Move. Kick*, he silently pleaded with her. *Do something*. But she lay there. Ian pushed his feet faster. Harder.

God, please help me make it in time.

What was the guy doing? Talking to her?

No time to think or care. He shoved into the man, knocking him face-first into the sand. Ian smashed the assailant's gun-wielding wrist with the driftwood. Cold waves washed the gun away as they splashed over them. The attacker grabbed Ian's throat. Ian pressed the driftwood against the criminal under him.

Which one of them would win?

The tide was coming in and another breaker slammed into them, tearing them apart. Hadn't he been through this before? But right now it was pitch-black on the beach, and he struggled to get his bearings. Prayed for a sliver of moonlight.

A flashlight beam shone bright.

Jonna. She directed the light so he could see the two men running away. "Cowards!" *Come back here*. Ian started to give chase. He wished for his weapon. He hadn't finished with them. He wanted, needed this to stop, to end right here tonight on this beach.

Jonna still lay in the sand. Waves would take her if she didn't get up and move. She must be injured.

He ran back to her. Dropped to his knees. The flashlight rested in the sand where she dropped it and provided just enough light for him to see her face was bruised and bloodied. And Ian's heart was crushed at the sight, the pieces clanking around inside him.

He cupped her face in his hands and peered at her,

looking into her dazed eyes. "I'm here, Jonna. You're going to be okay."

I told you, I'm a protector. But he hadn't protected her.

She didn't answer him, didn't show any signs that she had even heard him. He scooped her up into his arms. Strong Jonna, letting him do it. She was almost like a rag doll, dead weight in his arms, though her eyes remained opened.

What had they done to her?

The ocean took the flashlight, and wrapped around him up to his knees. It could have taken her so easily. He carried her forward and toward where he knew the staircase to the lodge to be.

Their plan had backfired so completely he wasn't sure how either of them had survived. He repositioned her in his arms, making sure her head rested against his shoulder. He had to make it up the slippery steps in the dark, so he gripped the rail as he held on to her and hiked up the steps. He couldn't know if the men would wait for them at the top.

God, help me know what to do.

I've failed so utterly tonight. I failed to protect her.

But even so, he wouldn't let go. How could he just walk away? He wouldn't give up. He wouldn't stop now unless she pushed him away. At the entrance to the lodge he rang the doorbell. Lisa let them in, a look of shock on her face. "What happened?" she asked.

He gave her a stern look. "You're to tell no one. No guests should know about this."

"I'll call the sheriff."

"No," Jonna said. "I'll... I'll call him."

Ian carried her down the hallway and unlocked the door to his own quarters. He considered taking her directly to his SUV and driving straight to the hospital, and maybe he would do that later, after they'd both had a minute to pull themselves together.

He kicked the door shut behind him. He didn't set her on the sofa, but instead eased both of them onto it, still cradling her in his arms. She didn't push away, but stayed there, seemingly content to be held by him.

"I need to take you to the hospital now."

"No. I won't go." Her voice was soft. Weak. He hated hearing her like this. "Just hold me."

Maybe she didn't want the word to get out. Or maybe this was the life she'd built and she refused to let these brutes take that from her. On some deep level, Ian understood—and he would give her that. It was her decision, after all.

They sat on the sofa together. Dawn came and went. Gray light of a stormy morning filtered through the mini blinds. Had she drifted to sleep? He wasn't sure. His body was bruised and aching, and he was sure she experienced the same pain. He would take it from her if he could.

Oh, God, please, let me take it from her. Let me protect her. Get this guy. Stop him. A quiet sob caught in his throat. *Why am I even here? She needs someone stronger, someone better than me.*

"Thank you, Ian." Her voice croaked. "You…you saved me again." Tears choked her words.

He never wanted to see her or hear her like this again. Never again. This wasn't the Jonna he knew.

"I didn't protect you."

"You saved my life—for not the first time. But…" She shifted away from his shoulder to look in his eyes, her face bruised. He wanted to reach up and gently touch the skin where those men had hurt her. Pain radiated over his body at the sight of her battered face.

Tears glistened in her eyes. "I saw you fall. I thought you were dead."

"I thought I was dead too. I landed on a tuft of land, a terrace hinging on the cliffside. After the Taser effects wore off, I climbed up in time to see them carrying you down the steps."

Her face—so beautiful even bruised—inched closer. Her warm breath feathered his skin. Her soft lips drew him. What would it be like to kiss her, to cherish her in his arms even for one moment? But that could go nowhere. *Focus on her eyes, man. Not her lips.* Tears clung to her lashes. "I couldn't let them get away with this," he said. "But they almost did. Jonna, I'm so—"

She pulled him closer and pressed her lips into his. He couldn't resist when Jonna kissed him, her lips sweet against his own. Emotion poured from her in this one simple act. Was this gratitude on her part? No, it was much more. When she eased back he deepened the kiss. He didn't want it to end, but she broke away enough to whisper, "You have nothing to be sorry for."

He didn't want to need this woman. *God, help me!* But he would kiss her back if that's what she wanted. He would kiss her as long as she'd let him. He sensed that both of them knew there could never be more between them and because of that, this kiss was bittersweet.

They were two of a kind.

And they were both broken.

TEN

Jonna let her lips linger, drawing in the essence of Ian. His goodness. His protectiveness. She'd thought she could watch over herself. But once again, Ian had saved her life. Still, she hated for him to see how weak she truly was. She'd had no power to save herself on that beach. Hated for him to see her so completely vulnerable, but she hadn't seen pity in his eyes. No. They had held something much more powerful.

In that moment, she'd known that she could trust Ian. How, she wasn't sure. She had known him for what— two weeks? And yet it felt like a lifetime. She had never wanted anything more, needed anything more, than to feel cherished and desired by this man. His kiss, his arms around her, holding her and caring for her for hours, had given her exactly that, except the kiss had unlocked a part of her heart she hadn't intended.

She wanted to be vulnerable with him, but had she scared him off with her forwardness? She couldn't take it back. Didn't regret it.

A heavy knock resounded, startling Jonna, breaking the connection with Ian. Her quick movement ignited pain in her head and body.

"It's DiAnn," the familiar voice spoke through the door. "We're looking for Jonna."

"I'll get it." Ian headed for the door.

Her protector.

"No, I'd better be the one." She slowly climbed from the sofa and inched her way toward the door, feeling every bit of the night's horrific trauma. She was fortunate to be alive.

More pounding. "It's Deputy Shane. Open up now."

Fury boiled inside. They were scaring her guests. "I'm coming!"

Ian beat her to the door. They had to stop the pounding and loud voices. He was thinking of her guests, as she was. He opened it wide so DiAnn and the deputy could see Jonna was all right.

DiAnn gasped at the sight of them. Deputy Shane pressed his hand over his weapon as if he would use it on Ian.

"Come in, and keep it down," Jonna said.

DiAnn and the deputy came into Ian's suite. He closed the door behind them, but the deputy kept Ian in his sights. His face raked over Jonna's haggard appearance— torn and muddied clothes, bruised face, tangled hair. "What's going on here?"

"I told Lisa not to call anyone. That I would call."

"Well, apparently neither of you called," Diann said. "But I did just as soon as Lisa told me. I'm sorry, Jonna. We were worried about you. We thought…" DiAnn glared at Ian. "Are you okay?"

Jonna stepped in front of Ian. "You have it all wrong. Ian saved me."

"From the Shoreline Killer? He tried to get you again?" Deputy Shane asked.

Easing into a chair, Jonna rubbed her face and was rewarded with another burst of pain, reminding her of the bruises. She must look a mess. "Are you taking my statement now? Because I don't have the energy to say this twice."

DiAnn knelt by Jonna. "Sweetie, don't we need to get you to a hospital?"

"I'm bruised, but otherwise fine." Truth was she didn't want people to see her like this. News might get out. Besides, as law enforcement in Miami, she'd been through much worse. "I don't want this story to go with the lodge and cling to it for years. Understood?"

"Yes, but you're more important than—"

"If I needed the hospital, I would go. But there's nothing wrong with me that can't be fixed with rest and time. If anyone asks, tell them I've taken a few days off."

DiAnn stood and nodded, clearly not agreeing with Jonna's decision.

"DiAnn." She waited until she had the woman's full attention. "I appreciate your friendship so much. I appreciate your ability to manage this place in my absence. And I'm trusting you to keep this to yourself. Share with Lisa and Kelsey, of course, but no one else."

"What about your aunt—"

"No one else."

"But she could come up here to stay with you and take care of you. Or you could go there."

"No one else." Jonna let her eyes make that clear. Her aunt didn't need the burden of worrying about Jonna. She'd been the one to nurse Jonna back to health when she'd come back from Miami. Aunt Debby had helped her get this lodge, keeping it in her own name for Jonna's protection. Her aunt had done enough. And going to her now would just put Aunt Debby in danger.

Her friend and employee pursed her lips, obviously torn inside. Jonna reached for her hand and squeezed. "Now, go ahead and go. I'll give my statement to the deputy if he's willing to take it. I'll be all right."

Her friend glanced at Ian, uncertainty in her gaze, but she did as Jonna asked and left the room.

"I'm ready to tell you about last night," Jonna said. "Please have a seat. It's a long story."

The deputy pulled out a notepad. "Since this involves the Shoreline Killer, I should call in the sheriff—"

"The Shoreline Killer isn't responsible for what happened to me."

The deputy slid into the chair at the table. "How do you know?"

Jonna blew out a breath, weariness heavy in her bones. She could sleep for a week. A month.

Ian busied himself making coffee with the small brewer provided in the suite. He'd been injured too, but he didn't let on. They could both definitely use the caffeine.

"Why don't I start from the beginning." Jonna explained about discovering her cabin had been searched and then coming up with the plan to stake it out, for which she received a reprimanding look from the deputy, but she ignored him and continued. She choked on tears when she told how Ian had been overcome with a Taser by the second man. A man they hadn't known about.

"We thought it was one guy, not two. We were caught off guard by the second man."

"I still don't understand why you think it wasn't the Shoreline Killer? He could have had help."

"Because, Deputy Shane, when I was on the beach incapacitated, right before Ian saved my life, right before the guy would have shot me in the face, I looked into his eyes. I have seen those eyes and that face before. Back in Miami. He is the same guy who left me for dead then. My past in Miami has come back to me—" *literally*, because she finally remembered "—and has caught up with me."

Ian set mugs of coffee on the table. Sliding Jonna's over to her, he kept his hand on the mug so her fingers would brush his. She shot him a glance, and he hoped she saw the reassurance he wanted to give her.

"Tell me about Miami," Deputy Shane said.

"You only need to know that someone tried to kill me there and now they've showed up here." Jonna's voice had grown stronger.

"Do you have a name? We need to put a BOLO out on this guy."

Shaking her head, she sipped from the mug. "No name."

"Do we have an image? Didn't you talk with a sketch artist in Florida?"

She rose from the chair and moved to the window, opening the mini blinds to stare out. "No... I... It's complicated."

"Try me," the deputy said.

"When I woke up in the hospital, I couldn't remember who shot me or even why. I guess someone thought I knew too much, but I really didn't know anything at all. All I knew is that I wanted out, so I pulled the IV's from my arm and left.

"For all practical purposes I disappeared. There was no reason for him to think I'd survived or to come in search of me. I'm not sure he was even aware of who I was—just a cop in the wrong place at the wrong time. My boss kept it all out of the news. But if you can get me an artist, I'll describe him now. Obviously he knows I survived. He knows my name. He understood where to look for me. I don't know why I would be worth so much trouble. They tried to take me out and make it look like it was the Shoreline Killer—obviously, because that's where our minds went from the start—then no questions would be asked, I can tell you that much."

The deputy stood, flipped his pad closed, his face vacillating between a frown and a scowl. Angry at what happened to Jonna? Or angry at her for keeping secrets? "I'm sure Sheriff Garrison will want to speak to you about this."

"He knows where to find me." Jonna hugged herself.

Ian gave the deputy a quick statement—he didn't have much more to add to Jonna's story—then ushered him out the door. The deputy leaned in. "You need to stay out of this and let us do our jobs. If you hadn't agreed to the stakeout with her, none of this would have happened."

Wow. What a slap in the face. "If I hadn't agreed to it with her, she would have done it herself. And then she would have died on the beach alone." Ian closed the door, effectively shutting off the ignorant deputy's reply. Sheriff Garrison would have understood why Ian had agreed to the stakeout. Their plan should have worked. They'd been blindsided by the man's partner. It wouldn't happen again.

He took a few seconds to gather his composure after the deputy's comment. Jonna remained at the window, staring out. He came up behind her. Another gray, stormy day. What was it about this weather that drew so many to this place? That had drawn Jonna? He hoped she would share that with him one day. "You should get some rest. Let your body and mind heal."

"I should check on Chop Suey."

"I can get the cat. Remember, he likes me. It's not safe for you there."

"I think we have a vacancy coming up. I'll move into that room. I don't want to trouble you. You've done enough."

Ian took her hand and led her to the sofa, where he gestured for her to sit next to him. "What happened back there? Will you tell me?"

She stared at her hands in her lap. "I will. Just let me sleep first. I'm so exhausted. You need to do the same, but I know you won't, will you?"

"I'll catnap while I have the chance. Don't worry about me." If only he could convince her to leave this place. To go away with him until it was safe to come back. Until someone had caught these guys. His gut tensed. He needed to tell her. Hated that he hadn't already. "There's something you should know."

She angled her head, concern in her gaze. "What is it?" He flinched a little at the suspicion in her tone.

Ian almost kissed her again to wipe that look off her face. He didn't want to see it, but he deserved it. He'd been at the inn quietly watching over her, quietly protecting her, and now he feared he was dangerously close to losing her. He feared he was going to fail to protect someone again.

And he'd waited too long, too late to confess his true reason for being there.

"Well?"

He drew in a breath. *God, please let her understand.*

"I was hired to watch over you and protect you by Gil Reeves."

Jonna's eyes widened. Anger flashed in her brown irises. "Why…why didn't you tell me?"

She rose from the sofa and stepped away from him.

"Uncle Gil asked me not to."

"Uncle?"

"That's right. He was worried about you. Knew you would never accept a bodyguard, so he sent me to watch over you discreetly. I've been trying to contact him to get his permission to tell you, but I can't get ahold of him. Now I'm worried."

Jonna glared at him, soaking in the news.

"Please understand, I *wanted* to tell you."

Oddly, hurt replaced the anger in her gaze. Ian took a step toward her. She held up her hand in warning.

"Jonna, believe me when I say I would be right here right now with you, even if Uncle Gil hadn't hired me. If I had known about you and about this situation, I would protect you anyway."

"It's who you are. I remember you said that."

She had him there, but the reason he stuck around to watch over her was so much more than just his basic protective instincts. Admitting those reasons out loud to Jonna wouldn't do either of them any good. He would do well to stick to the fact Uncle Gil had hired him.

And forget the feelings, the strong draw she was to him. Disentangle himself from the power she had over him—power she wasn't even aware she had. But that power was too strong. Would he be able to escape?

And could he protect her? Or would he watch her die? He couldn't go through that again. If someone had to die, Ian would make sure he was the one.

ELEVEN

Jonna hugged the pillow in the crisp, clean bed of the recently vacated suite. Having finished prowling the new-to-him room, Chop Suey snuggled next to her. She ran her fingers through his soft fur, sending some of it floating, drifting off, per usual. She'd have to do some serious vacuuming in here, which she did anyway, especially when a guest brought a pet with them for their stay.

Every part of her ached, including her heart. She should fire Ian. Send him home if she could. But she couldn't really fire him when she hadn't hired him. She could kick him out of her lodge. But she knew he wouldn't go far from her. He would just sit in his SUV down the road. She couldn't do that to him.

Why should she feel so hurt and betrayed that he'd known so much about her and never told her? He'd only been doing his job. But she supposed it had more to do with disappointment in herself that she'd allowed herself to care. And...she'd kissed him! If she could only take it back...

He was only doing his job—watching over her.

What a fool she'd been to let him under her skin. When would she learn?

Jonna didn't have the time or energy to suffer like this, yet here she was suffering, emotionally, psychologically and physically. Somehow she had to get her act together. But she couldn't do that without rest.

God, please let me fall asleep! It was only 10:00 a.m., but she'd been up most of the night.

Pushing aside thoughts of Ian and the connection she'd thought she'd had with him, she focused on her lodge. Her heart ached—the peaceful way of life she'd carved out for herself had come to an end. The man—or men, there had been two of them—who had left her for dead back in Florida had finally come for her. Why? What had happened? It had been three years since she'd left Miami and her job there.

Three years.

True, she'd made no effort to change her identity, but she hadn't believed someone would risk exposing themselves by coming after her when she was no further threat to them, for all practical purposes.

She'd walked away last time—yielded the ground and left without looking back. But this time she wouldn't run away. She would stay and fight. And she had to get over the pain in her heart. She thought she could trust Ian. Even so, she'd never intended to let him into her heart. They'd spent long hours together. Shared so much, and the whole time he'd kept his real reason for being at her lodge to himself. Ian wasn't far removed from a liar as far as Jonna was concerned.

Except…well…he'd only been doing his job. Admittedly, she would have done the same. But it went much deeper. He claimed he would protect her, and despite wanting to keep her distance, she had taken that to heart as though he cared about her personally. He'd kept that he was a *paid* protector from her.

She'd known better than to let her guard down. This whole time and Ian was nothing more than…well…

Her secret bodyguard.

Jonna finally slept, though bad dreams accosted her. She woke up feeling groggy. She'd slept the whole day, though, because it was already dark again outside. The clock said five o'clock. The wind beat against the windows. She spotted her gun on the side table. Would her attackers try again tonight?

She thought someone would wake her if the sheriff wanted to speak to her. Had Ian spoken to him on her behalf?

What was the guy doing now? He needed his rest too. But she had no doubt he had found a way to watch over her. To guard her. Gil Reeves was paying him to do it, after all.

She tried to get angry about that again, but the fury just wouldn't boil to the surface.

Maybe that had to do with the image imprinted on her mind of him being incapacitated by the Taser and then shoved out to what should have been his death. He'd protected her with his life.

Multiple times. Would a hired protector who was only doing his job really go that far?

She couldn't help but think Ian cared as a friend, and maybe something more, but maybe she was only fooling herself again. She shoved from the bed to take another hot shower. Either way, Jonna wouldn't open up her heart again. She would forget the kiss. Forget how he'd made her feel cherished. Forget the deep pools of blue in his eyes.

Jonna groaned. Now the anger came, but it was with herself. She quickly showered so she could be ready to sit and wait the night out. No way could she sleep. She doubted the guy could so easily find her in this room, but she wouldn't risk it. Flipping through the news channels, she realized she was hungry and called up to the front desk.

"Hey, Lisa."

"Oh, hi, Jonna. Are you okay? Do you need anything?"

"As a matter of fact, I'm sorry to bother you, but if there's anything left in the kitchen, I could use some food. I… I don't want to come out until my face looks better." And just how long would that take? A week or longer? She had to come up with a better plan.

"Sure, I think DiAnn is here with something for you. She said something about preparing a tray."

A soft knock came at the door.

"Oh, I bet that's her bringing me something. Thank you. And Lisa, I appreciate your concern."

"You're not mad that I told DiAnn you were hurt and we called the deputy?"

"No, I'm not mad. It's going to be okay. *I'm* going to be okay. Just don't tell anyone else."

"You got it. Good night, Jonna."

More knocking, but still soft and not impatient like earlier in the day when DiAnn had come with the deputy to look for her.

"Coming," Jonna called. Then thought better of it. She grabbed her weapon from the side table. "Who's there?"

"It's me," Ian said.

Jonna frowned. Was she ready to face him yet? She couldn't decide if she preferred him or DiAnn with a tray of food. But she couldn't get rid of him or ignore him so opened the door.

Ian held up sacks. "I thought you might be hungry."

Okay. Well. How could she deny Ian *and* food? She opened the door wide and waited as he walked by, his musky scent swirling around her head. She reminded herself that she remained disappointed in him for not telling her the truth.

He glanced down at her weapon. "Still mad at me, huh?"

"Oh, this?" She examined it. "I wouldn't want to waste a bullet." A tenuous grin pulled at her left cheek. "I'm only kidding." *Sort of.*

DiAnn appeared in the doorway carrying a tray from the kitchen. "Oh, I guess I should have asked. I didn't realize you already made plans."

She turned to walk down the hall.

"DiAnn," Jonna called. She leaned out the door and motioned the woman back. "Let me have the tray. I'm famished. I didn't make any plans. Ian just showed up. He was being thoughtful just like you."

Diann handed her the tray. "All right, then. Let me know if you need anything else." The woman eyed Ian, apparently still distrustful.

Jonna leaned closer. "He's saved my life three times, DiAnn. You can trust him."

Her friend and employee frowned slightly but nodded. "Okay, then. You know best." She inched away, then headed up the hallway.

Jonna shut the door.

You can trust him...

She'd given the advice to DiAnn but wasn't willing to follow it herself. Then again, maybe she could trust him with her life. Just not her heart.

Ian struggled to look at Jonna's face, but hid his reaction. At least she looked more rested. More in control. And more guarded.

He couldn't blame her there. She felt betrayed. That was all on him.

Inwardly, he sighed. Outwardly, he tried to smile when he'd rather frown. He hadn't asked to be put in this position—to become the betrayer. But he knew that was how she saw him now. After opening the sacks, he spread out the Chinese takeout he'd had delivered to the front entrance. He spread the small boxes of sweet-and-sour chicken, fried rice, beef and broccoli, and a few egg rolls on the small table. "Mind if I join you?"

"Suit yourself." Jonna pulled a chair out for herself and started in on the tray DiAnn had brought—beef stew and bread—then eyed the Chinese food. "Nothing compares to Asian spices swirled in sugar and fat. When did you get this?"

"Not long ago. It's still hot."

She pushed DiAnn's tray away and offered him a soft smile. Were they friends again?

"Just so we're clear," he said, feeling daring enough to tease her a little, "this isn't the dinner I owe you."

"You don't owe me anything, but this can count as dinner. It…it was thoughtful of you. Thanks, Ian. I'm starving."

"That's a good sign."

They ate in an awkward silence. Ian had things to say and suspected Jonna was holding back too, but they should eat first. Get their strength back. Move beyond this uncomfortableness.

After a few bites, she finally said, "I hope you got some sleep."

"I got enough. I talked to the sheriff this afternoon." In addition, Ian had taken the time to comb the beach, search around the house to see if one of the men had left evidence behind. The weather wreaked havoc on that possibility. Then Ian had taken a three-hour catnap and he was good to go.

"And?"

"Tomorrow we'll go see him. We'll meet with the sketch artist if you're still up for that."

"Definitely." She finger combed her long, still-wet hair, now free of the sand and salt. He could smell the fruity shampoo from across the table.

Thoughts of her kiss hijacked his mind. Emotion pulsed through him. He calmed his heart. Steadied his mind and pulled his gaze from her hair.

Ian worried about tonight. What if there was another attack? How could he protect her if she kept her distance? Refused to work with him? How did he get back into her good graces?

"You look…better." Good wasn't exactly the right word, though to him, Jonna was beautiful no matter what. He tried to hide how much seeing her like this affected him.

They'd grown close and then he'd shattered it with the truth, but that was for the best.

She huffed an incredulous laugh. "I look like something from a horror flick. You're not going to win points with more lies."

He chafed at her remark. Ian had to be careful what

he said next or he'd put even more distance between them. "Listen, Jonna, I never wanted it to be like this. I didn't want to keep it from you. I've wanted to tell you, and I tried—"

She held up her hand, gesturing for him to stop. "Save it. You don't need to keep apologizing. You saved my life, Ian—over and over again. And I can't thank you enough. I just… It burns, you know? This whole time you were here and knew things about me, and you were watching me." She pushed the plate away as if she'd tasted something bad.

"If I could have gotten ahold of Uncle Gil and gotten his permission to come clean then I could have told you sooner. Right now, I'm worried that something has happened to him."

"I emailed him a couple of days ago," she said. "I haven't heard back either. A couple of weeks ago, he had called to tell me that my name came up in some chatter. Three years and nothing. Now they hear my name. He didn't know what it meant, but told me just to be careful. Then you checked in at the lodge. You were fortunate to even get a room. You know that? It's been a slow season. I think that's because of the Shoreline Killer, honestly." She frowned and studied him. "I'm worried about Gil too. What do you know?"

"I've repeatedly texted, emailed and called. I finally called his assistant at work."

"Who is it? Gerry?"

"No. Nadine is her name."

Jonna frowned. "I don't know her. What did she say?"

"That Gil is at a conference. Then I called back today to ask her to speak with Gil's coworkers at the conference to make sure they had seen him. That he's actually there. I'm still waiting to hear back."

"I don't want to go down this line of thinking that he might be missing. I really don't want to be concerned like this. He's probably busy, like Nadine said."

"Jonna, my messages—the new ones, anyway— explained that it was urgent. That you had been attacked. If he was checking his messages at all then Uncle Gil would respond to that no matter what."

Her brows furrowed. "Let's say something has happened to him. What are you thinking that could be?"

Ian hung his head, shaking it. "Let's just hope someone at the conference says he's actually there. But if I hear back otherwise, I don't know what to think except that someone needs to search for him. If that's the case, Jonna, would you consider going back to Florida with me to find him? It would get you away from this lodge and the danger here."

"You want me to go back into the lion's den?"

"No. It wouldn't be like that. Those men are here to find and hurt you. They would never expect you to go back to Miami."

"I made a decision last night that I wouldn't run again. I wouldn't walk away from the trouble I'm in this time. I would stay and face it and neutralize it. Maybe then the dreams from the past will quit haunting me. But you... I think you should go find Gil. I'm worried about him too. Please keep me informed."

This time Ian couldn't hide the hurt that exploded. Could she really send him away that easily? Even if he had severed the emotional connection—a good thing in the long run—didn't she put any value on the way they'd worked together to keep her safe?

"No. I won't leave you here to face them alone. You know the sheriff's department or the state police can't give you the kind of protection you need. Yes, you need protection, Jonna. Even with your skill set, you need backup. If you won't come with me then I'll stay here. We'll get them together. Uncle Gil will be all right."

If he was in some kind of trouble, someone would figure it out and help him. Ian wouldn't abandon the woman he'd promised to protect.

Funny about that. When had he made that promise to himself?

TWELVE

The next day, Jonna sat in a room at the county sheriff's department, talking to Susan Staples, the forensic artist they'd brought in. Exhaustion interfered with her ability to accurately describe the man's face, even though it was forever etched in her brain.

Now…now that her memories of that day in Miami had returned, seeing him again had triggered it to all come rushing back.

Ian stood back in the corner, leaning against the wall with his arms crossed. Last night they reviewed the lodge's security footage and came up empty. Then they'd taken turns staying awake and on guard in case her predators returned. The perpetrators hadn't shown up. She was relieved, but only to a point. That could mean they had come up with a new strategy to get to her. And next time, she'd have no way of knowing how or when they'd strike.

A chill crawled over her.

Describing the guy sent her mind right back to that moment when he pulled the trigger, three years ago in Miami. It was terrifying. No wonder her mind had so thoroughly blocked the details. But now she relived it.

A warm, strong hand gripped her shoulder. Ian said nothing, but his reassurances came through his touch loud and clear.

She closed her eyes. Tried to picture every detail she could think of about her attacker's face as she described him.

"Okay," Susan said. "I think I have it. Tell me, is this the man?"

She held up a detailed sketch.

Jonna recoiled as images from last night and from Miami pummeled her.

Ian took a step toward her. She subtly eyed him, warning him off. She would be okay.

Gathering her composure, she slowly nodded. "That's him exactly. Even the look in his eyes is right."

"I'll give this to the sheriff and, who knows, they could have him in custody by the day's end."

Jonna wished she could be that enthusiastic, but this man had lived in the criminal world much too long. It wouldn't be that easy.

"Are we free to go now?" Ian asked.

"Let me ask the sheriff," Susan said. "He might need to talk to you."

Jonna pressed her face into her arms on the table. Ian pulled up a chair to sit next to her, much too close. He acted like he was more than a bodyguard. The problem was, Jonna didn't mind. She needed him. More than she would ever have thought. But she couldn't need him too much. Had to protect her heart.

God, how do I do that?

"I'm sorry you had to relive that moment again, Jonna," he said.

She lifted her face to gaze into eyes much too blue,

and almost wished she hadn't. "How did you know that I relived it?"

"I've been there. There's a moment that I relive far too often."

Oh, Ian... She pressed her small hand over his much larger one. Felt the warmth there. She wished there was something she could do to wipe away those memories for him. To ease the pain.

"You really need to forgive yourself, Ian."

Dimples formed in his cheeks as they lifted. "Maybe I will at some point. But I don't want to talk about me now. Will you tell me what happened to you?"

Oh, God, I don't want to think about it. I don't want to go there again. Help me! "I've tried to forget for so long, but it keeps coming back in my dreams. Everything except his face—that was the part I could never remember. And then I had to see it again two nights ago." Jonna tried to keep her voice steady, but the way Ian looked at her, she could tell he saw too much. He saw right through her.

She owed the guy her life. He'd nearly been killed while helping her, and yet he was still here with her, wanting to protect her. His being here might have had to do with Gil hiring him to begin with, but somewhere in her heart—a place he'd somehow penetrated—she knew that Ian was here for his own reasons. That didn't help her efforts to protect her heart.

"You know some of it, I'm sure. What did Gil tell you?"

"I want to hear it from you, Jonna. Please help me to understand."

He wanted to feel her pain with her? She could see it in his eyes. "Telling you won't take it away from me, you know? I'll still carry it with me."

"Maybe it will help."

Whatever. She needed to talk to someone. Who else could she turn to? Ian would understand to some degree what she'd been through. "All right, but let's get out of here first. I can't sit in this hard chair or stare at these blank walls anymore." She needed to see the ocean.

He scooted from the table. "I'll be right back."

A few minutes later, he returned. "The sheriff had to leave. He got a lead about the Shoreline Killer up the coast. They have what they need from you, Jonna. Let's go."

In Ian's SUV, Jonna let her mind drift. For the first time since this started, she allowed Ian to be the one to watch and worry, if only for a few minutes. They'd checked his vehicle for GPS trackers before taking it out. But by now, her predators knew their pattern. The thought dragged her mind back to her morning jog. She hadn't been jogging since this started.

Ian drove through a coffee kiosk where he purchased two coffees and blueberry scones. He shot her a grin. "I'm sure they're not as good as the ones at your lodge."

"We can compare and see." But she was absolutely sure she wouldn't be able to taste anything.

Then he parked the vehicle at a viewpoint along the coast.

"Why are you stopping here?" she asked.

"I didn't want to take you back to the lodge just yet. I thought you might like to watch the storm."

"And tell you what happened."

He nodded. "If you're willing."

She let the coffee warm her, the scone comfort her, the crashing waves soothe her. "You're right. I don't think these scones are as good. That's a load off my mind." She offered an incredulous huff. As if eating the scone could remove an ounce of her burden. Still... "Thank you, Ian."

"For what?"

"For this. You're thoughtful, I'll give you that."

He said nothing, but patiently waited for her to tell her story.

"We were working on a human-trafficking ring. I spent two years on that case. The atrocities I uncovered I can never forget. What we humans are willing to do to each other—" Jonna shook her head. "We finally had enough evidence on the key players to bring most of them down. But not *all* of them. I suspected someone politically connected was involved. But I was told we were closing in and making our arrests. I had nothing on the senator. Just... An informant gave me this shell—the one I had in the closet in my cabin. He kept telling me about the shell company. We looked into the money trail, believe me, but they'd done a masterful job of covering their tracks. Nor did we have enough for a warrant to look into Senator Shelby personally. Add to that, the department was pressured to close the case and make arrests without further delay."

"Let me guess, Shelby pressured them."

"No. The mayor. His constituents wanted to end the scourge of human trafficking. Gil was only following orders. We arrested six men and four women for their crimes. The press called us heroes. The mayor even presented our department with an award at the annual gala.

"But I wasn't done yet. I wanted evidence to bring that last player in. I couldn't be sure Shelby had anything to do with it, but my gut told me there was more there and I couldn't let the case go. I knew even if I had evidence, he would likely still go free, but I wanted answers. On my own time, I kept looking. That day, I'd followed a clue to an abandoned warehouse. It wasn't secluded, but in the industrial district, working through everything that had happened—it was like I could see it all playing out in my head. How the girls were brought in from foreign countries. The horrible things that happened to them. Going over it again. I remember hearing someone behind me. I turned around and…he used a Taser on me. Just like he did the other night.

"I was taken to a marsh several miles away and thrown out. I had no chance of running. He shot me." Jonna placed a hand over her midsection. She edged up part of her sweatshirt so Ian could see the scar on her abdomen. Tears choked her next words, but she continued. "I'd been shot before, but this was different. I was left to bleed out, to die, in the marsh. I'm surprised an alligator or some other creature didn't find me, with all that blood. It was beyond painful."

Ian reached over and took her hand. He squeezed it tenderly, but said nothing. What *could* he say?

"I woke up in a small county hospital. They didn't know who I was. All my identification had been removed. I'd been unconscious for days, but was healing. I knew then I wanted out. I don't know if that man shot me because I kept digging into the trafficking case. But why go to the trouble to dump me in the marsh? If I couldn't bring justice to the man ultimately behind the trafficking ring, then I was done. I could never win against the powers that be. And if that was the case, I would disappear quietly into the night. Maybe I was a coward to leave. Maybe I was weak."

"No, Jonna. Never say that about yourself. You're the strongest person I know."

Well, that made two who thought that—Ian and Aunt Debby. She laughed and sniffled. "I pulled out the IVs. No one was around. I took some nursing scrubs and walked out of the hospital. Came back to my aunt Debby's here in Washington. I called Gil and explained that I was resigning. If someone wanted me dead that badly, let me stay dead. Gil agreed that if I couldn't remember my attacker's face, I'd be a walking target if I stayed there. He made sure the hospital billed the insurance and took care of all the loose ends.

"After nursing me back to health, Aunt Debby took out a loan to buy the inn. She's the owner on paper, but it's mine. I just wanted to remain in obscurity. Work through the pain in my own way. Fast-forward to three years later and here we are. I kept dreaming about what happened, but I could never see his face until he was at the beach. Why now, Ian? What happened that made him come back for me?"

"I guess that's the kazillion-dollar question. I think we need to look into this guy—Senator Shelby. See what's up with him now, if he has any reason to want someone to kill you."

"You're right. I should have thought of that, but I guess I didn't want to believe it. It's just so surreal that any of this is happening." She fumbled with her smartphone.

"Here, I'll look it up." Ian stared at his phone and typed. Paused as he read the search results. "He's running for office again."

"Yeah. Of course he is." That must be why he wanted someone to close up any loose ends—so she couldn't interfere with his reelection. But she never had any evidence. Just the cryptic clue from her informant.

Ian lifted his face. His blue eyes had turned dark, matching the stormy Pacific. "I don't think these guys plan to go back to Miami until they finish the job here. It sounds to me like they were led to believe you were dead three years ago—the guy who'd been hired to do the job had told them so. But maybe it came to light that you were still very much alive. I'm thinking that maybe this guy who was supposed to kill you has been taken to task because he didn't complete his job. Maybe it's your life or his now."

She leaned her head against the passenger window as she stared at the waves she'd always loved. Then she let her gaze fall on Ian. "Then I guess you have your work cut out for you."

At her words, his throat tightened. He turned to face her again, aware she was studying him.

"After all, your uncle hired you to protect me, didn't he? So the question is, Ian Brady, are you up to the task?"

He'd hoped to see amusement in her eyes. Her beautiful brown eyes held a challenge in them instead.

And that was good because she should be taking this very seriously. But Ian wasn't sure how to answer that question.

"I think it's time for you to tell me what happened when you were a federal agent with DSS. I mean, what *really* happened. I told you my story. Now you tell me yours."

"Oh, is that how it works?"

"Yes. That's how we play. Are you game?"

Her sudden edgy playfulness had him smiling inside,

even though he really didn't want to reconnect with her in that way. Still, he was happier than he should be that the playful banter they'd previously enjoyed had returned. "I guess I can tell you, but then you might not want me to protect you. And, Jonna, this isn't a game."

"*Au contraire.* It's a game, all right. It's a deadly game." Her chin jutted out and fire blazed in her brown eyes. "I might have walked away before, but I'm standing my ground this time. I have no intention of letting them win. So tell me now what happened before. I want to know about the man I'm trusting to have my back in this."

He swallowed the lump in his already-tight throat. "Fair enough.

"Before I was DSS I was an MP. Military police. That qualified me to work as a special agent in the Protective Liaison Division. I provided protection to diplomatic missions and consular posts." He glanced at Jonna, hoping he hadn't lost her. But she appeared to be keeping up. "Foreign missions, we call them."

"Wait. What is the difference between DSS and the Secret Service? It's kind of embarrassing that I don't already know that."

Good question. "Secret Service takes the heads of states."

"Like presidents."

"Yeah. And kings. Prime ministers. The bigs. And we cover the next tier of VIPs. Those who are equivalent to, say, our secretary of state. Foreign ministers. Anyone who is an internationally protected person. We once protected the Dalai Lama."

"And what's your story?"

"I can't tell you names. I can't reveal that kind of information."

"That's fine."

"I was working to coordinate the protection detail for a foreign minister and his family out of our New York field office."

"What was her name?"

Her question took him aback. "What was whose name?"

"The woman you fell for."

"I didn't say anything about a woman."

"You didn't have to. I can see it in your eyes. This story involves a woman you fell for."

"I hadn't fallen for her."

"But you wanted to."

He hesitated. He'd already hidden too much from her. Might as well tell her everything. "Yes. She felt the same about me. Maybe I *did* fall a little."

Jonna's expression appeared pained. Hurt. Jealous maybe? But concern for him quickly overran all other emotions in her gaze. "More than a little, I'd say. What… happened?"

This was the part where it got hard to talk about it. "Communication is one of the most important parts of a protection detail. A measure of security is based on knowing every possible threat. She didn't tell me she had someone else. Someone from home. But apparently she'd told him about *me*."

Jonna sucked in a quiet breath. She probably guessed what was coming. But he still needed to say it.

"She…she was killed."

"Oh, Ian. I'm so, so sorry."

They sat silent for a few long moments. His failure entailed so much more than failing to protect the diplomat's daughter. His heart twisted up inside.

"If I had known there was a threat of that nature, I could have better protected her. But her family didn't approve of the jealous man she'd been seeing. Her father bringing her to this country was meant to remove her from her entanglement with him, so the family was careful to never mention him, hoping she'd forget. She was to become betrothed to another important man in another country. So you see, she and I, we were never meant to be. And in the end, not only did I fail to protect her, I caused her death to begin with."

"That's a lot to carry. I had no idea, though I should have suspected it would be something complex. But, Ian, please, you can't blame yourself for what happened. It was all much bigger than you and beyond your control. Sounds like the guy would have killed her anyway before she married the man her father had picked for her. She was doomed from the start."

"She wore a necklace he'd given her. It had a tracker on it so he could keep tabs on her. He got it from a British jeweler who creates what he calls fidelity engagement rings to keep track of spouses. He hadn't told her about that feature. She couldn't tell me what she didn't even know herself. Still, I should have prevented it. I should have known."

"I'm sure you did everything you could, given the circumstances. Have you…have you ever tracked someone like that? In order to protect them, of course."

What was she getting at? "You mean, without their knowledge?"

"Maybe."

"No." She'd given him an idea. He eyed her, searching her gaze. Did he see fear? Uncertainty? "Let me have your phone."

"What? Why?"

"I'm going to put a tracker on you, with your permission. One I can easily follow with my own phone."

"What? No necklace?" She feigned disappointment.

A laugh almost escaped. "Would you like one?"

"I was only kidding. If someone was able to get the upper hand and grab me—take me away from my protector, say—it's likely I wouldn't have my phone with me. And even if I did, they would just toss it."

"I'm doing everything in my power to protect you. This is just a start. I can put other things in place if you'll let me. I'll work on that when we get back. But we can start with your phone here and now."

"Thank you." She placed her hand over his, sending that familiar charge through him—even in the midst of this tragic story of his past failure to protect a woman… might as well admit it…a woman he'd loved.

Now was the time for him to make things perfectly clear between them. "You're welcome. But you understand now why I can never let myself become distracted again while working a protection detail." *Or otherwise…*

Jonna must have read his message loud and clear because she slowly removed her hand. Hurt was flickering in her gaze, but something more too. Understanding.

They were in agreement, then.

Ian's cell rang. Gil's assistant. He quickly answered.

"Ian, you were right," she said. "I'm sorry to have to tell you…but no one at the conference has seen Gil."

THIRTEEN

"Oh, no. Oh, Ian… I'm so sorry." For all of it. For the woman he'd lost, and now the more pressing issue—Gil.

Jonna sat up, wishing there was something she could do. She felt so helpless.

Ian stared at his smartphone and squeezed it so tightly she thought it would break. He shifted his SUV into gear, backed out and peeled from the parking lot, his tires spinning against the wet pavement.

"I should have known something was wrong the first day he didn't answer. I should have made them look for him then."

Jonna held on as he whipped the SUV out onto the road.

"So you're going to Miami now to look for him?" Should Jonna go too?

Oh, God, I don't know what to do here. Help me to know.

"And leave you here to face off with killers? No. I can't fail Uncle Gil—protecting you was the last thing he asked of me, though I think it had as much to do with encouraging me as helping you. You're my first job as a freelance security consultant, Jonna. I didn't know if

I'd be able to do this job after failing so badly before, but Uncle Gil believed in me and trusted me with someone he cared about—you. I'm not going to let him down."

"You must be torn about this," she said. "Gil wouldn't insist that you continue guarding me now that I know about it, for one, and if he needs your help, I think you should go." A pang hit her chest. She didn't want Ian to leave. But she knew it was for the best for a thousand reasons, not the least of which was because neither of them were relationship material. She was a distraction for him.

He was a distraction for her.

"Would you even consider a safe house an option, Jonna? Because unless you're willing to go into hiding for now, then I'm not leaving you."

"Even if you're not under contract anymore?" Oh, why had she asked that?

"I prefer to think Uncle Gil is still alive, if you don't mind. About your question—I think you know the answer to that."

Jonna watched the beach and waves speed past as the vehicle moved down the road, then trees hide her view of the ocean. Yes. Yes, she did know the answer. Ian would still be here protecting her, whether he got paid for it or not, because she was in danger. And then when that danger was gone—he would leave.

"I don't want to get in the way of you finding your uncle. Let me think about what to do, okay? Pray about it."

"Pray we find my uncle, Jonna. Pray that law enforcement catches the men after you, now that they have a sketch. They might even have a name soon too."

His knuckles were white as he squeezed the wheel,

steering the SUV around curves in the two-lane coastal road.

"Do you think it's possible that his disappearance has anything at all to do with what's happening here in Washington?" she asked.

"I don't know." His voiced sounded strained. "It's possible."

"But is it likely?"

Ian passed a vehicle and an oncoming truck honked as he swerved quickly back into his lane.

"Do I need to drive?" she asked.

"No. I'm sorry. I'm just worried about Uncle Gil."

"Well don't forget you're protecting me and that means driving safely." She wasn't sure why he was speeding back to the lodge unless he intended to high-tail it back to Miami to find his uncle.

He immediately slowed the SUV. "I'm sorry, Jonna. Forgive me?"

"There's nothing to forgive." She watched out the passenger-side window. Glory rays shone through a break in the clouds and beyond that, dark clouds moved in, bringing another series of storms.

Jonna had left one storm in Miami to live what she'd hoped would be a peaceful life, but it had turned out to be a metaphorically stormy existence. *The irony.*

"So let's review what we know," she said. "Gil gets some intel and my name comes up three years after I left Miami. He calls to warn me to watch my back, but the danger seemed minor. There wasn't any real warning in his voice. You show up. Two weeks after you show up, someone tries to kill me on the beach. After that, you and I both tried to get in touch with Gil to let him know what's happening. Attacks on me here continue."

"And we know it's not the Shoreline Killer, but the man who shot you before," Ian said. "It appears they wanted it to look like it was the serial killer to cover their tracks and not lead authorities back to Miami and open an investigation, which would cause them more trouble. Then today we learn Uncle Gil, your old boss, is missing, and has been for days." Anger edged his voice. Anger and fear.

Jonna could hardly stand to hear that coming from her protector. She wished she didn't care about him on a deeper level. Somehow she had to put that aside. Otherwise maybe someone would get hurt because of her, just like someone got hurt because of Ian. She didn't blame him for drawing the lines. She had drawn them herself for different reasons. Only problem was she kept crossing those lines.

"I think it's highly possible that Uncle Gil's disappearance is related." Ian parked the SUV at the lodge. He searched the area, as did Jonna.

"What now, Ian? What do we do?"

"If we could catch these guys here in the next day or two, then we might get answers from them about Gil. If not…" He let his words trail off.

She knew what he would say next. *You go into a safe house and I head to Miami.* Ian didn't know her well enough yet if he didn't know that she would go back to Miami with or without his permission. At the thought, Jonna's heart pounded as though she had some sort of PTSD. Maybe she did. Maybe she really couldn't go back and face what she'd left behind, even though a huge piece of what had driven her away had followed her here anyway.

"Are you ready?" she asked.

He pursed his lips, clearly upset. Then a sharp focus came into his dark blue eyes, the color shifting again. Lighter blue as he stared at her. She understood—he was focused back on protecting Jonna. Warmth flooded her. And not a little guilt—Gil could use Ian's help. Could use Jonna's help too.

"Yes. I'm ready. Stick close."

For the first time, Jonna found herself not reacting negatively to the fact she needed protection. She struggled to discern the difference between needing it and wanting it from Ian specifically—with his dark, shaggy hair and eyes that made her heart flutter like some school girl. She hadn't thought in her thirties that anyone could have that effect on her. She wished Ian didn't move her, but he did. Unfortunately, she wanted to know more about the woman he'd fallen for before. The daughter of a foreign dignitary. Jonna imaged this woman to be beautiful and elegant. Refined and glamorous like Jonna had never been. She could totally imagine Ian with a woman like that. Jonna could never be someone who could make him happy.

She'd just have to find a way to stay alive, capture the bad guys, find Gil and control her emotions while working with her not-so-secret-anymore protector.

The once beautiful thick woods of hemlock and spruce hedging the lodge had now turned dangerous. Killers could be hiding in the dark forest. The security consultant in Ian chafed at this inadequate protection scenario. His nerve endings on high alert, he watched the woods and the surrounding area as he ushered Jonna into the main lodge entrance.

When this first started, her demeanor had shifted

and she'd carried herself more like the previous law-enforcement officer she'd been, only she'd been leery of trusting anyone to have her back. But now Jonna walked closer to him, appearing to accept his role in her life as a protector. That was good. All good, but part of him hated what was going on that forced her to rely on him, and yet another part was relieved that at least she trusted him to protect her. Though he would avoid it if possible, he still had a feeling it would take their combined skill set to see this through. They'd had a couple of close calls, but he believed they worked well together, like partners who had been working together for years. Still, that scenario worked best when one partner wasn't a target.

Even the best team could fail, though, and he and Jonna had both come close to losing their lives. Regardless, Ian couldn't think about his recent failures protecting Jonna. He needed to concentrate on the here and now. At least the close call had reset Jonna's memory. They had a face now. Maybe would get a name soon.

Before she entered the room where she stayed now, he would make sure it was safe, and clear her cabin too. He didn't like that her permanent dwelling served as a back entrance into the lodge. He needed to set up a solid security system complete with cameras before the end of the day, if possible. It didn't take his skills as a security consultant to see this setup was far from ideal in terms of safety and protection.

Ian wasn't sure how far these guys would go to hurt her. They might take drastic measures, now that their previous attempts had been foiled.

His only reassurance was that he didn't think they would target an entire lodge and plant a bomb. That would draw the attention of multiple agencies and the feds. He doubted the person behind this would want that kind of attention.

Once they were through the door, the wind and cold fell away and warmth engulfed them. DiAnn offered a tenuous smile and rushed forward to greet Jonna.

"What's wrong?" Ian asked.

"Can we talk?" She kept the smile in place but led them down the hall to Jonna's room.

Ian insisted the women let him go in first to clear the room. DiAnn gave him a strange look. "What's going on? Why does he have a gun?"

Jonna closed the door. "Ian is a security specialist. He's here to protect me."

The woman eyed him with suspicion. Nothing new there. Once the room was cleared, he tucked his weapon away.

"What's wrong, DiAnn?" he asked. "What's happened?"

Diann crept over to the window and peered out. "Lisa told me this morning that someone's been hanging out around the lodge. A stranger. So when she left this morning I watched for him."

"And you saw him?" Ian asked.

She nodded slowly. "He's over at the restaurant a lot."

"Did you tell Deputy Shane?"

"Yes. The deputy went to the restaurant and had coffee. Said he didn't see anything suspicious about the guy but to let him know if something else happened."

Ian ground his molars but kept his expression even. The guy could be innocent, but if he raised the suspicions of Jonna's employees, it was worth taking the warning seriously. Surely Deputy Shane had seen the sketch artist's picture and would know if this was the man who tried to kill Jonna. Still, there had been two men, and they didn't get a great look at the other one.

"And has anything else happened?" Jonna asked.

DiAnn hugged herself. "About an hour ago he came into the lodge to ask if we had any vacancies."

Jonna visibly paled.

"And what did you tell him?" Ian peeked through the mini blinds, eager to get out and search for the guy, but first he needed to gather all the facts.

"I told him no, of course. Jonna took our last available room."

"And he seems suspicious to you why?" Ian needed to hear her impression.

"I don't know exactly. Maybe because he leans against the wall across the way watching the parking lot. Watching the lodge, incessantly smoking. It's cold outside. Who wants to be out in this weather?"

"Do people usually stand out there?"

"Well, not usually. I guess they do when the weather is nice. I can't say that no one ever stands there. But for hours on end, hanging around? It just seemed odd, and given everything that's happened, it's disturbing."

Ian agreed it warranted checking into. If it was one of their attackers, then he'd brazenly shown his face, which seemed unusual. Why would he do that? "What did he do after you told him there was no room at the inn?"

"He left the counter and went into the storm-watching room with the big windows and fireplace. I tried to stop him but he said he wanted to look around."

"Then what did he do?"

She pursed her lips. "He sat in one of the chairs and made himself at home. I didn't know what to say. I didn't want to make a scene in front of our other guests."

"Do people who aren't guests usually come inside to watch the storms?"

Jonna pressed a hand on DiAnn's arm to let her know she would answer. "Yes. They eat at the restaurant next door, but to get the best view they often come over here. We've always allowed it. It's a way of promoting the lodge. Sometimes that experience converts into them booking a stay in the future. We send people to the restaurant and they send them over here."

Made sense. "Is he still here?"

"He left right before you got here, but he could still be out there watching."

Ian peered through the mini blinds. "Thanks, DiAnn. Let us know if you see someone else."

The woman didn't appear ready to leave. "What's going on, Jonna? I think you owe us an explanation."

Brows furrowed, Jonna closed her eyes as if to organize her thoughts. "You're right," she said. "We think this has to do with my past. I was in law enforcement before coming here, you know. More than that, I really shouldn't say."

"Do you think anyone else is in danger? Those of us on staff? Guests at the lodge?"

Pain exuded in Jonna's gaze. Had she considered that possibility? Time for Ian to step up.

"I don't think anyone is in danger other than Jonna," he said. "These men want to keep it low-key and avoid drawing too much attention to themselves." But obviously they were stepping up the tempo now. Ian would have a word with the deputy and see if he'd asked the guy for an ID. Run his plates. Anything at all.

"If you're a security specialist, or a bodyguard, please protect her."

He read DiAnn's expression clearly enough—she thought he'd fallen down on the job, considering Jonna's purple face that she'd tried to hide with makeup. Unfortunately, he couldn't disagree with her.

And—why hadn't he seen this man when they'd driven up? If the man was waiting for them, Jonna could be in imminent peril even now.

When DiAnn left, Ian paced the room. Uncle Gil was missing. The men after Jonna were closing in. He rubbed his temples. All he wanted to do was take her in his arms and kiss her. A completely inappropriate response. He wished they were through this. He wished they had neutralized the threat and that she was safe and Ian had protected her so they could just spend time together without any risk. But that wasn't going to happen. When this was over, he had no reason to stay. No reason to remain in her life.

Jonna came out of the bedroom with her weapon.

"We should check the security footage," he said.

"I have a better idea. Let's go get answers from him."

FOURTEEN

Admiration flashed in his eyes before he shuttered it away behind an intimidating frown.

"Whoa." Ian put up his hands. "*We*, Jonna? I don't want you anywhere near danger. I made that mistake already and you nearly died. I won't make it again. If it were up to me, we wouldn't even be at this lodge right now."

She hid the Sig away in the holster beneath her jacket. "Get real. I'm not going to hide away in some safe house. You know I'm going with you. Before we get too close to this guy, I'll know if it's someone I recognize from last night, or even from Miami. And what—are you going to leave me here unprotected instead? We know he's not working alone. His partner could attack me here while you're occupied elsewhere."

At the intense blue in Ian's gaze, his complete silence, Jonna stepped closer to emphasize her resolve. Only problem was, she couldn't stare him down. He was much too tall.

She didn't want to look at his lips or his strong jaw or think about how it had felt to kiss him. Jonna refocused her thoughts. He was such a distraction.

She knew what Ian needed—reassurance. She would give that to him. "I trust you to protect me, Ian. To do what your uncle hired you to do. But the best way to protect me is to get to these guys first. I have skills. Take advantage of them. There's no point in waiting around for them to attack again. Agreed?"

She stood so close to him now. Why had she approached him like this? What was it about Ian that drew her? He looked down at her. Pain and turmoil were fighting with reason in his expression. She recognized those emotions all too well.

"Let's do this together," she said, as persuasively as she could. "And then...then we'll go find your uncle."

Oh, she was playing underhanded now. Manipulating Ian.

It didn't go unnoticed.

He arched a brow. "So that's how it's going to be, is it?" The hint of a dimple appeared.

And she wanted to kiss him. To be in his arms. Her heart betrayed her head—no way could she fall for this guy. They could never be together. If she didn't know that already, he'd been the one to make that clear earlier.

She took a step back. "Yes, that's how it's going to be."

He tugged out his weapon and examined it. "Just remember, this wasn't my idea. But I appreciate that you have skills, Jonna. Let's hope we don't need them today."

"Even so, I hope this lurker is someone who can give us answers."

"I want to clear your cabin first, make sure no one has been there or is hiding there." Ian led the way out of her room.

Jonna followed him. An unexpected result of shifting back into law-enforcement mode was that she realized she missed certain aspects of her old job and old life. Not enough to go back into it full-time, but the job had challenged her and given her an adrenaline rush at times. She'd felt like she was accomplishing something valuable by bringing down the bad guys, but when the system worked against her and justice didn't prevail and she'd been left for dead, Jonna had needed out.

No guests were in the hallway, for which she was grateful as she used her key to unlock the hall entrance to her cabin. Ian pushed in first, his weapon at the ready, and he filed in to the right. Jonna followed him, coming in low and to the left. They were an odd couple—acting as though they were partners in law enforcement. Still they had a good rhythm together.

Her cabin clear, Jonna searched again to make sure no one had been back in here to look through her things.

"I'd like to set up a good security system and cameras as soon as possible," Ian stated.

"I have the bare minimum in place," she said. "It's what came with the lodge. I hadn't thought more was needed." Maybe it had been more that she hadn't wanted reminders of just how bad crime could be. She'd hoped and believed she was safe here on the coast. For years her aunt never locked her doors. Jonna had been fooling herself, wishing for the good old days that were now long gone.

She locked up her cabin's entrance to the lodge and they exited through the cabin front door, which put them outside.

Jonna and Ian remained on guard, looking for their attackers. The woods provided too much cover to someone who wanted to lurk and watch. She didn't much feel like tromping through them at the moment in the cold, even though the wind had died down and only a light misting rain coated her cheeks. Ian's much-larger form protected her as he escorted her around the lodge.

They searched for the suspicious man.

Was he there with ill intent? Or was he just an innocent guy who'd accidentally drawn her employee's attention?

After a thorough search of the parking lot, they headed for the restaurant, Ian continuing in a protective stance. Admittedly he could only shield her so much, given the area. Just as they approached the restaurant, a man came around the far corner.

He looked down as he walked. Pulled the hood on his coat tighter. He appeared smaller than the two from the other night. Was this the lurker? Was he involved with the men after Jonna? Ian walked slightly ahead of Jonna, shielding her with his body—she wasn't entirely sure how she felt about that. If something happened to him because of her, she wouldn't get over it.

Suddenly the man twisted around and walked the other way.

"Hey," Ian said. "We want to talk to you."

He took off.

"Hey!" Ian called, and gave chase. Jonna was right on his heels.

Whoever this man was, he wouldn't have started running if he didn't have a reason. Definitely suspicious activity. He ran across the street, darting in front of a car that honked and swerved.

Ian and Jonna slowed to wait for a truck passing on the two-lane road.

"He's heading into the woods," she said. "What if others are waiting?"

Through the trees, they spotted him getting away. Ian sprinted and Jonna kept up. They jumped over brambles and fallen logs. Dodged boulders.

They reached the edge of the woods and a Windsurf neighborhood sprawled before them. Ian slowed long enough to catch his breath.

Jonna was there with him. "See. This is why…I jog… every day."

He bent over his thighs. "You knew this would happen?"

"I didn't know it then. But I know it now."

A form dashed between cars up the street. "There."

They jogged up the sidewalk and when it was safe, cut between cars into the neighborhood. *God, please keep us safe. Keep Jonna safe.*

"He jumped over that fence two houses down." Ian's breathing became too labored. He could run a marathon, but he couldn't keep up this sprint for too much longer.

"He's taking the short cut. There's no way for us to catch him." Her words came out between breaths.

"Unless we know where he's heading."

"I don't think he knows where he's going. Just trying to lose us."

"Hey." A man came around his house. "You the cops or something?"

Ian and Jonna shared a look. "Close enough," he said.

"The guy you're chasing? He took off across the street. I've seen him a few times already. Thought he looked suspicious."

"Thanks," Ian said. "Was he alone?"

"A couple of times, yeah. Then another time he had a big guy with him."

Ian handed off his card. "Please call us if you see them again." They headed across the street to search.

Jonna took the lead this time, more familiar with the neighborhood. "He must have been cutting through those woods to the lodge to watch us."

Ian scrutinized the area ahead of them, and what they'd left behind. "Remember, there's more than one of them. Maybe we should head back, Jonna."

"And admit defeat?" She paused to catch her breath. "We work well together, Ian. I think we can get this guy."

"If we haven't already lost him."

Dogs barked a few houses down. Again they shared a look. Together they took off running. "The way those dogs are barking, sounds like they have him cornered," Ian said.

"Let's split up. I'll go around this way. We can come at him from different sides."

Images from their previous attempt to corner what they thought had been one man working alone accosted him. "Not happening. We stick together."

Between two houses, they crept to the back. A vicious snarl from behind and much too near sent lead into Ian's legs. He turned to see a German Shepherd approaching.

Slowly, Ian pushed Jonna behind him.

Had the man released someone's guard dog to distract Ian and Jonna?

"Ian?" she said his name haltingly. "What are we going to do?"

"You're going to call 9-1-1, for starters. I'm going to deal with the dog."

"But—"

"Shh…"

Behind him, Jonna made the call. Ian cautiously crouched. "Hey, buddy."

He didn't make any threatening moves or give the dog a reason to attack him. Instead, he slowly offered his hand.

Jonna was on the phone. "Yeah, the suspect is getting away. We're back here cornered by a German Shepherd. I have no idea how to get him back where he belongs. Please help!"

The neighbors were obviously not home.

Teeth and another snarl pressed against the fence behind them. Jonna jumped closer to Ian.

The dog in front of them inched forward as if to sniff Ian's hand, his snarl softening as he sniffed.

"Wow, Ian. What are you? The guard dog whisperer?"

"Cujo, stand down!" A male voice shouted. Then the speaker rounded the corner from the front of the house. Brows furrowed, he eyed Ian and Jonna. "I've called the deputy."

"He's already on his way," Ian said.

"Yeah, that's what he said. He told me who the two of you are—that you can be trusted—but he didn't say what had happened. What's this about?"

"We were chasing down someone. Your dog got in the way."

The man grabbed Cujo by the collar. "I'm so sorry about this. The guy you were chasing must have let him out."

In the distance, tires squealed and metal crunched. The man's gaze jerked toward town. "Sounds like a wreck."

"Well, we'll just be going. You can let the deputy know you saved us when he gets here."

The man eyed Ian's weapon. "I appreciate you not shooting my dogs."

"I wouldn't do that." Unless the dog attacked Jonna. "Might think of putting a lock on that gate."

Ian wanted to question the guy about why he had two attack dogs in his backyard in this nice, homey neighborhood. But it was a free world and as long as he kept them under control, that wasn't against the law. "Let's go."

Jonna followed him. They jogged down the street, looking for their guy.

"We lost him, Ian. He's long gone now."

They made the crosswalk near where the car wreck happened. A crowd had gathered. Jonna and Ian hurried to offer aid. Sirens rang out. An ambulance picked its way through the traffic.

Shock rolled over Ian. On the street, his body broken but still breathing, lay the man who'd shot Jonna in Miami.

FIFTEEN

Ian tried to shield her, but Jonna brushed his efforts off and rushed forward, approaching the man who'd been hit by a car, the collision having caused another accident. The two motorists were out of their cars and looking on in horror. The man lying in the street appeared to be the only one seriously injured. An ambulance steered through the crowd. The deputy they'd called jogged toward them.

She couldn't believe it. This man was the same one who'd shot her in Miami. Who'd left her for dead. Who'd tried again to take her life last night. She thought he was unconscious, but he groaned. His lids fluttered. He locked gazes with her, knocking the air from her lungs. She stumbled backward, but strong hands held her steady.

Ian.

Jonna crouched near the man. "Help is on the way. You're going to be okay."

He gurgled words. Blood dribbled out. Her heart went out to her would-be killer.

Clearly he wanted to tell her something.

"Back. Get back. Please move out of the way." The authoritative words came from behind her.

EMTs. The deputy.

She was running out of time to hear what her attacker had to say.

The man gripped her hand, startling her. "I thought… you were dead. In Miami." He gasped for breath. "When I knew you weren't…didn't tell anyone."

Why was he confessing now? Did he want redemption? *God, please let this man survive!*

Fear and grief squeezed her chest.

"Found out you were. Alive. Sent me. To finish… or else. Boss. Gil Reeves. In hospital. He…won't last… They'll kill."

Seconds ticked by before she comprehended his words. Gil was in danger. They would try to kill him in the hospital. Her heart palpitated.

Oh, God! Please protect Gil.

This man wasn't going to last either. She had this one chance to get more information. "Who? Who is behind this? Who is trying to kill me?"

Again his words were garbled. The bitter taste of acid rose in her throat. She leaned closer.

"Mayor Hendrix—" His eyes glazed over.

"What did you say?" When she looked at him again, lifeless eyes stared back.

Grief squeezed her insides.

He was going to say something more, but what?

Time morphed into a slow-motion movie reel as the EMTs took over. Jonna was escorted away from the man and the crowd.

Ushering her aside, Ian had his arm around her. Something about the way he held her bothered her but she couldn't figure out why, since one thing pushed all other thoughts aside.

Mayor Hendrix...

It couldn't be.

"Breathe." Ian's blue eyes stared into hers as he slightly crouched to eye level. "Breathe, Jonna."

"I'm okay."

"No. You're not. You look like you've seen a ghost."

"I…"

"What did he say? Did he tell you who's behind this?"

"Ian." She searched for the words to explain but they wouldn't come. She had to tell him…

"That's it. Let's get back to the lodge."

Again, he wrapped his arm around her. Though he held her gently, she could feel the power, the strength in him as he hugged her tight and walked with her. The way he held her felt almost…personal…but he'd been hired to protect her. Even though they'd shared a kiss, this wasn't personal for him. It couldn't go anywhere. They both knew that.

Two other men after her remained out there.

And Gil.

She shuddered as the images from Miami, and the images from the beach here, accosted her. She'd thought she was so strong on her own. So capable. But she'd been blindsided. The blow to her face suddenly throbbed. Her limbs ached. She was on the beach thrashing and then unable to move from the electricity that shut down her body.

Jonna didn't remember getting back to the lodge. Or even sitting at the table in the room where she was staying.

Ian handed her a big mug of hot coffee. "Drink up."

She sipped the black brew. He pulled out a chair, sat next to her and set his Glock on the table. Arms crossed,

Ian watched her. The concern pouring from his gaze nearly undid her. What was this thing between them? She had no business letting him into her heart, but it seemed Ian was getting under her skin without her permission.

"I have to hand it to you," she said. "You're being very patient."

He arched a brow. "I'm concerned about you. How can I protect you if you won't tell me what's going on?"

Unfortunately, Jonna liked the sound of his voice. The words he said about protecting her. She'd never thought she'd want or need protection. Maybe it had nothing at all to do with protection and everything to do with Ian.

She forced her thoughts back to more pressing matters.

"He gave me a name, Ian, when I asked who was behind the attacks on my life." She took a drink.

"And?"

Jonna set the mug down much too hard on the table and cringed. "I'm having a hard time with it. The name he gave me. It's not who I suspected. I don't know what to think."

Ian looked at his smartphone. "What's the name? Let's see what we can find on him."

"Mayor Hendrix."

His expression grim, Ian set the phone back on the table. "I guess there's no need for me to look him up, then."

Ian scraped both hands through his hair. Reached for his gun. Bolted from the chair and paced the room.

For some reason, his reaction didn't surprise her. He worried about how he would protect her, given the VIP involved. Was there more than one? Back in Miami, she'd suspected the senator of involvement. But never the mayor, who had celebrated in their success at shutting down the ring.

Ignoring the pain from their confrontation with bad guys, the stress of the last many hours, she forced herself from the chair to block Ian's path as he paced. "Ian, stop."

He stilled. His brow deeply furrowed as he looked at her. She wanted to reach up and run her fingers over his face to soften the worry. Remove it from him if she could. That's what she got for caring about him. Or letting him care about her.

But none of that mattered right now. They had much bigger problems. He didn't know the worst of it.

"I have an idea." She would be proactive with the delivery of the news that would affect him most.

His gaze bored into hers. "I'm not sure I want to hear it."

"Sure you do." She stepped closer, took his hand. His strong, capable hand. She held it gently to deliver the news. "The man told me your uncle is in the hospital. He's in danger. They're going to kill him, Ian." His eyes widened as he tried to pull away, but she held tight. "We're going to Miami. And while we're there, we're going to take down the man behind the attacks. I don't care how big and important he is. It's time for me to stop hiding, to stop running and to start hunting."

His blue eyes turned dark, a brackish gray. "And you expect me to protect you."

She nodded. "You're the only one I trust with the job."

"You know that's not how it works," he said. "I can't protect you if you're going to make yourself an easy target."

He steadied his breathing. Controlled the emotions at the news she'd delivered. The good news was that, if the guy could be believed, his uncle was still alive and was receiving the required care in the hospital. But was he getting the protection he needed?

What had happened? The man behind the attacks on Jonna was obviously involved. Ian had yet another reason to want to get at the bottom of this and take the man behind this down.

She watched him, waiting for him to say more.

Holding his hand, using her personal connection to him, the woman *and* the former ICE agent peered into his eyes now, pleading. Her big brown eyes made all the sharper with well-defined brows. High cheekbones, supple lips that he could never forget kissing—all that determination and tenacity wrapped up in this lovely package. It was hard to resist.

Someone pounded on the door. Ian whipped around, his weapon ready. "Who is it?"

"Sheriff Garrison."

They'd left the scene without talking to Deputy Shane. But Ian had needed to get Jonna back to the lodge for her protection—both physical and emotional.

Lowering his weapon only slightly, Ian strode to the door in two steps and opened it.

"Mind if I come in?"

He opened the door wider, allowing the sheriff to step into the room. His law-enforcement presence made the space seem small.

"Jonna." He dipped his chin. "I take it you already know, but one of the men who attacked you died today.

His name was Danny Johnson. Does that mean anything to you?"

She shook her head. "When he was dying. Before he died... I...talked to him."

The sheriff seemed surprised by that news. "Deputy Shane didn't tell me."

"It was before he got there," Ian added.

"Have a seat." Jonna pulled out a chair.

"I'll stand, thank you." Sheriff Garrison whipped out his pen and pad, ready to write.

She took the chair.

"Are you going to tell me what was said?" the sheriff asked.

Would she tell him about the man's accusations regarding the mayor of Miami?

"He told me that Ian's uncle was in the hospital and his life was in danger."

Sheriff Garrison arched a brow and glanced at Ian. "My uncle was Jonna's boss at Homeland Security. He's the one who hired me to protect her."

"Sheriff, we were chasing a suspicious character. Someone who had been hanging around the lodge. We planned to question him but he took off running. He wasn't one of the two who'd attacked us last night. We called Deputy Shane when we ended up being trapped by someone's guard dog. My point is, we weren't chasing Danny. But maybe they were planning to ambush us. There are two other men, as far as we know, still out there."

The sheriff's mouth twisted into a deep frown as he scribbled on his pad, then tucked it away. "I think it's time for you to get out of town, Jonna. Can't you go to your aunt's?"

Her expression turned indignant. "And put her in danger too? I don't think so."

The man turned his fierce gaze on Ian. "You're protecting her. What are you going to do about this?"

Ian gazed at Jonna, her brown eyes expectant. "I think we're getting out of town." Jumping out of the firestorm into the war zone.

"Good. By the way, the man with the guard dog? That dog is trained to track. He got a scent on the man you were chasing. So we're going hunting this afternoon."

"Good," Ian said. "If you can keep those two guys who are after her here and on the run so they won't follow us to…wherever we're going…all the better."

"How soon are you leaving?"

Jonna shoved from the chair, still a little unsteady on her feet. "Within the hour. I need to let my staff know I'm leaving for a few days. I don't like to leave my lodge—" the truth of that showed in her eyes "—but it isn't safe for anyone without law-enforcement experience to be near me until we get these guys. I appreciate all you're doing, Sheriff."

Sheriff Garrison thrust his hand out to Ian.

The sheriff's grip practically crushed Ian's in the handshake. "Take care of this woman. I get the sense that you're the kind of man who is willing to give your life in the line of duty." To Jonna, he said, "And you, Jonna. You let him do his job."

Sheriff Garrison's radio squawked, and he responded, bid them goodbye and left the room.

"I should go pack," she said. "As should you."

"We'll stay together. I'll wait for you to pack."

Jonna gave him a soft smile. "We'll protect each other."

"I wouldn't trust anyone else with the job." Ian returned her smile and ignored the warning signals going off in his head.

SIXTEEN

Was this a bad idea? Ian peered down the aisle of the Boeing 737 that was carrying them to Miami, after a connecting flight in Denver.

Even if it was the absolute worst path they could have taken, what could Ian do to stop Jonna? She'd go to Miami on her own—exactly what his uncle had been afraid she would do. Uncle Gil hadn't wanted Jonna to get back into the middle of a perilous situation. But Uncle Gil hadn't known how widespread the firestorm would be. Staying in Washington wouldn't keep her safe.

The only option left to Ian was to stay by her side.

And protect her. *We'll protect each other,* she'd said. While he trusted her on that, it wasn't her job to look out for him. And she was making his job all the more difficult. Still, they'd worked well together from the beginning, and maybe they could continue to work well together.

He released a resigned sigh.

He'd called Gil's supervisors, who'd located him within hours of learning he was missing. Fortunately, they already understood the need for a guard next to his hospital room. But Uncle Gil was in bad shape. If only it wouldn't take Ian and Jonna a day to get to Florida from Washington with the connection and time change.

The flight was completely full. He'd set the air above him to blow directly on him and push away the stuffiness. He sipped iced water from a plastic cup. Next to him, Jonna sat quietly reading an airline magazine, but he suspected she was busy strategizing in her head what they would do once they arrived in Florida.

Go see Uncle Gil first. That was a given.

Except if Gil was being watched; then in doing that, the person who wanted her dead would know she was back in town.

Was it Mayor Hendrix? Jonna had said the dying man acted like he meant to say more. What if he hadn't been blaming the mayor at all? They couldn't just waltz in and accuse the man.

Somehow, though, they'd have to find out if he was in it up to his ears or if he knew something that could help them. Ian's uncle would have been the best person to discuss the details with, but the man had been badly beaten. He remained in a coma for who could say how long.

God, thank You that Gil is in the hospital and not lying in some ditch somewhere to die alone. But please, help him get better.

He took a sip of his water.

Jonna flipped the magazine closed and stuck it into the seat flap. "So, Ian. Tell me about the woman you fell in love with."

He choked, sucking water down the wrong way. He could have spewed it over the seat back.

"Are you okay?"

He shook his head, unable to speak yet. Why in the world was she asking that question? And now, of all times. He'd assumed she was thinking about what came next. What they would do once they got to Miami. But she was thinking about Serena?

He pinched his nose.

"I'm sorry. I shouldn't have asked that. You don't have to answer if the subject is too sensitive."

"No. It's okay. You just surprised me. Why do you want to know?"

"Forget it. It was a stupid question."

"Not stupid, just surprising. That's all. Let's make a deal. I'll tell you about Serena if you tell me about the last guy you were involved with."

She shoved her long hair behind her ears and grabbed the magazine again. She'd already looked through it twice. "You know, this conversation is off-limits. It's too…personal. Again, I apologize for asking to begin with."

Ian closed his eyes and pictured Serena. Unfortunately, the image elicited a massive explosion of pain—taking an interest in her had resulted in a tragic domino effect on many lives. Deep-seated regrets over his mistakes could throw off his game when it came to protecting Jonna.

"I imagine she was very beautiful," she said, her voice a soft whisper.

So they weren't done with this yet. Keeping his eyes closed, an image of the woman he'd cared deeply about appeared. "Yes. She was." *But not as beautiful as you, Jonna.* He shouldn't tell her that. They shouldn't take their attraction, their connection any further. *She was not as strong as you are.* Or skilled. Not as smart or as self-sufficient. Still, there were similarities. Both had tender hearts that they fiercely protected.

He never would have believed that caring for someone could bring so much death and tragedy. He couldn't do that again to anyone.

Jonna pressed her hand over his on the armrest. Behind the softness, he felt the strength in her touch. Why was she doing this to him?

But that wasn't on her. His reaction to her was on him.

She was simply being herself—a caring, sensitive woman. Once they arrived in Miami, Ian had to remain focused on one thing—protecting Jonna.

You're the only one I trust with the job.

He hoped she wasn't making a mistake.

As the plane descended for a landing at Miami International Airport, Jonna stared out the window, her old stomping grounds rushing at her both physically and metaphorically. Her mouth went dry as her pulse kicked up.

What would it feel like to step foot in Miami again?

Unwanted memories came flooding back with more clarity than ever before.

She tried to slow her breathing. Maybe coming back was a mistake. But what choice did she have? Someone—Mayor Hendrix, possibly—had targeted her. Did he think she knew something, or had evidence against him? If she did, she would have come forward long ago.

She had only suspected someone in authority was involved in the human-trafficking ring, and she'd believed the culprit to be Senator Shelby. Her informant had been trying to tell her something. Had she misunderstood? Maybe that was it—they thought her informant had told her. That's why she'd been targeted. Apparently Danny had told them he'd finished the job and killed her. But someone had obviously ratted on him that Jonna was very much alive and well. Jonna was a loose end.

No, she was much more than a loose end—she was more like a loose cannon.

A loaded weapon.

I'm coming for you...

First she had to find out if Mayor Hendrix really was the man behind targeting her. If not, then who?

As they exited the plane into the terminal, dizziness swept over her.

Ian grabbed her hand. Tugged her over into a corner and out of the flow of people. "You okay?"

"Yeah. I just never thought I'd be back here."

He gently gripped her arms. Peered into her eyes. "Listen, Jonna. We can leave. You don't have to do this. In fact, I'd prefer you didn't. I'm ready to go with you anywhere you want to go."

"And forget about your uncle? My old boss whose only crime was to try to protect me?" She leaned against the wall and drew in a breath. "I have to do this. But you're the one who doesn't have to. This isn't your fight. You don't have to go into this with me."

Was that hurt flickering in his gaze?

She offered a tenuous grin, then gently took his hand and squeezed. "You know I want you with me. I just don't know if I could live with myself if something happened to you." She pressed her finger into his chest. "So don't get hurt, Ian. Don't die to save me just because your uncle or the sheriff made you think you had to." Did she even hear herself? She was the one putting him in danger by being here. "Come on. Let's go see Gil."

They hurried through the terminal with their carry-on bags, Ian holding her arm, keeping her close. Both of them watching the crowd for anyone suspicious who might be tracking them. The one thing they had going for them was that whoever wanted Jonna silenced wanted it done discreetly. They would likely continue to try to kill her without witnesses, and in such a way that it wouldn't be traceable back to them.

Half an hour later, Jonna followed Ian through the white, sterile hallway of the hospital where his uncle—her former boss—was recovering from his injuries. He'd been abducted from a conference in Georgia, and too many hours had passed before anyone realized he was no longer there. During that time, thugs had beaten him for information. He was fortunate to have made it out alive.

Ian faced two police officers stationed outside Gil's hospital room. "Ian Brady here to see my uncle."

"Can I see some ID, sir?"

Ian showed the man his ID. Jonna did too. The officers allowed them into the room.

"Gil, you're awake!" Jonna rushed to the bed ahead of Ian.

Gil's face was black-and-blue. His eyes and lips swollen. It reminded Jonna of her own face, only his was much worse. Gil looked at her and anger flashed in his eyes.

He ground out the next words, directing them at Ian. "What is she *doing* here?"

SEVENTEEN

Ian could barely recognize his uncle. Seeing the bruises and the swelling nearly undid him. Hearing the fury Uncle Gil directed at him filled him with shame. He measured his next words, but before he could respond, the man continued.

"They beat me to find out where she was. I never told them. I was prepared to give my life before I told them. I endured that, Ian, so you could protect her. And you bring her here? To Miami? Right back into the hornet's nest?"

"Gil." Jonna's soft tone drew the man's attention. "There's something you don't know."

"I'm listening."

A nurse came into the room and frowned. "Mr. Reeves, you need to rest." The nurse eyed Ian and Jonna. "I'm afraid I need to ask you to leave."

"No," Uncle Gil said. "I need them to stay until I get answers." His authoritative tone silenced the nurse.

She didn't argue further. But she injected something into his IV. Something to help him relax or sleep?

Ian hadn't meant to upset his uncle. They hadn't even known he'd woken from the coma. Ian had only wanted to see him and make sure he was okay. He wanted his uncle to rest and recover, but there were things they needed to share with the man. Maybe even a few things Uncle Gil could tell them as well. He wished he could stay here and watch out for his uncle. He wasn't sure the man was safe, even here in the hospital.

Two people he cared deeply about were in danger.

When the nurse exited the room, Gil said, "Tell me, Jonna."

"The man who shot me in Miami showed up in Washington and tried to kill me."

Uncle Gil groaned. Maybe they shouldn't tell him this. He tried to catch Jonna's attention, but she forged on. Besides, it was too late now.

"He had two men with him—that we know of. There could have been others. Since they were watching me, they must know by now that we left the area. Sooner or later, they'll find out I'm here in Miami, but I don't think they know yet. I have a short window in which to take advantage of that. So we need to act fast."

Uncle Gil's face paled and he shut his eyes. Something the nurse put in his IV working? But he opened his eyes again. "I didn't tell them. At least... I don't think..."

"Gil," Jonna and took his hand. It was almost as if they had shared more than a simple professional relationship. Maybe Uncle Gil thought of her like the daughter he'd lost? That must be it.

"It's not like Jonna changed her name or her appearance," Ian said. "It wouldn't take that much digging to find her if someone was determined."

"The lodge is in my aunt's name, legally, so I'm not that easy to find. Still, why would they target me? I don't know anything. If I had any evidence, I'd have turned it over three years ago. All attacking me is going to do is make me angry, and I'll be sure to find who is behind this."

"Putting yourself in more danger. I had hoped Ian would protect you."

"And he has. I'm starting to lose count of how many times he has saved my life," she said. "You sent the right man. That said, Ian can't protect me from myself." She offered a wry grin—for his uncle's sake, Ian assumed.

But Uncle Gil didn't pick up on it, his frown deepening.

"Uncle Gil, do you know anything that can help us?"

"Help you what? You are not going to investigate. You are not going to try to find this man, Jonna. You aren't an ICE agent anymore. Even if you find out who's after you, you can't arrest him. This isn't your responsibility."

"You want me to go into hiding and do nothing? I did that already. It didn't work. Besides you sent Ian to protect me. Don't you trust your nephew?"

Uncle Gil's gaze drilled into him. "I trust him implicitly. I believe in him. But he can't do the impossible."

Though true, his uncle's words knocked the support beams he'd built out from under him. He had no adequate words with which to respond.

"This is a fool's errand." Uncle Gil turned his bruised face away from them.

"Don't blame Ian," she said. "I'm here because they found me in Washington. Hiding won't work. I have to finish this or I will forever be looking over my shoulder. Ian has no choice. If he wants to protect me then he has to be here in Miami with me."

Uncle Gil remained silent for so long, Ian thought he'd finally dozed off. Then the man shifted his face back to them, his expression revealing the movement was painful.

"Tell us what you know." Jonna crossed her arms, putting her soft side to rest. "Do you have any thoughts about who is behind this?"

He gave a subtle shake of his head. "I only know that three years ago Mayor Hendrix put pressure on the higher-ups to close the case. We don't answer to the mayor, but in this case, we did what we were told. We didn't have any evidence of a money trail leading to anyone else beyond the people we'd already taken into custody. But you...you didn't let it go."

"And now we know why someone shot me. It was related." Jonna told Uncle Gil everything Danny Johnson had told her with his dying breath.

"You can't go after the mayor, Jonna. What are you thinking?" Uncle Gil asked.

Jonna moved to stare out the window. A thunderstorm brewed in the distance. Uncle Gil once again glared at Ian. Sure, love resided behind that glare, but the man felt helpless to save those he cared about, which Ian completely understood. His uncle could lose two people he cared about in one fell swoop if Jonna remained determined to solve this—and pulled Ian into the line of fire along with her.

"I wish I trusted someone with this," Uncle Gil said. "Someone else who could help. But obviously this thing goes deep. If a VIP is involved, I don't know who I can trust. Someone knew how and when to take me. Who knew I'd be at that conference?" He released a breathy sigh. "What about you, Ian? Can you call in some old DSS buddies? Is there anyone you can trust?"

"Maybe." Ian had someone in mind. He'd been considering making that call today. "Jonna and I wanted to see you first. We've been so worried about you."

"I don't know if anyone told you," she said, "but Ian was the one to put pressure on them to find you. Everyone in your office thought you were at the conference, and the people at the conference thought some work emergency had made you leave."

"I was sure you would have responded to my communications about Jonna." Since Gil had been abducted, it was likely his abductors had seen at least the texts Ian had sent. No matter. He hadn't revealed anything other than Jonna's location in Washington, which the bad guys already knew. "I was so worried about you—" he shared a look with Jonna "—*we* were so worried."

"Well, you've seen me. I'll be okay. Now, get her outta here. This is too open. Too obvious."

Once again, Ian endured his uncle's scolding, then the man's gaze softened. "I told you, didn't I? I warned you about how stubborn she is." His uncle ended his words with a smile. And then Ian was certain that Uncle Gil thought of Jonna like his own child—she was so much like Ian's late cousin Stephanie, Uncle Gil's daughter.

He read too, the stern message in his uncle's eyes.

Protect Jonna and stay alive...

Ian at her side, Jonna strode down the white halls as if on a mission and watched for signs of men with ill intent. They needed a plan. A solid strategy. All she could think about was getting to the mayor. Surprising him. Maybe he was innocent. Maybe not. But being wired while she met him and told him Danny's words might getting him talking. She could angle for a confession.

But she had to convince Ian to go along with it, and that would be a hard sell.

They entered the elevator with several other visitors. One serious-looking man made her nerve endings crackle, and she watched him in her peripheral vision.

Maybe Gil was right. Her attempt to get to the bottom of this was a fool's errand.

In the elevator, people shifted around as more crowded in. Others got off. Next stop, they ended up alone with the suspicious man. She couldn't say exactly what it was about him. It was only a gut feeling.

Tension rolled off Ian. He must sense it too.

His fingers tickled hers, then slid completely around her hand, grasping it. The elevator dinged. A nurse and a woman with an empty stroller got on. Ian quickly pulled Jonna out and ushered her down the hallway.

"This isn't our floor," she muttered.

"I know."

She glanced over her shoulder. "He's following."

"Figures."

Great. She'd been made. What had she expected? Ian tugged her around the corner. A nurse had opened a set of double doors with her keycard—Hospital Staff Only. Ian yanked Jonna through and into another long corridor.

"Hey!" the nurse yelled.

Ian continued ushering Jonna away from a man who meant her harm. He pulled her into a closet left unlocked. The pungent odor of antiseptic seized her. He locked the door and flipped off the light. In the small space, they remained silent and motionless, hoping the thug had lost track of them.

Jonna held her breath. She suspected Ian did too. Her heart pounded so hard, she thought he would hear it. She'd lost her ability to control the panic in situations where she needed to have her game on. Finally, she gasped for breath, revealing her fear.

In the dark closet, Ian reached for her and pulled her against him. "It's going to be okay."

His reassurance steadied Jonna. He wrapped his arms around her. Her head against his chest, she heard his strong and steady heartbeat. Jonna shouldn't, but she relaxed against him. If only she wasn't damaged. If only they could truly be together. She could imagine herself in his arms forever.

The doorknob twisted. Someone grumbled. Keys jingled. Jonna instinctively reached for her weapon. But of course she didn't have it. Couldn't carry a gun into a hospital.

The door swung open. A woman opened her mouth to protest at the sight of the trespassers, but Ian prevented her from doing so by yanking Jonna out of the closet and down the hallway. "Let's hope we lost him," he said.

They hurried down the hall and took another staff elevator along with two hospital orderlies pushing a bed on wheels. Ian's demeanor said he had every right to be on this elevator. Then Jonna noticed he'd snagged a nurse's keycard and it hung around his neck so he looked like hospital staff. Though under normal circumstances she would frown on that behavior, this was a matter of life and death. She trusted he would return it to Lost and Found later. But right now, it kept others quiet while they made their escape through the staff-only elevators.

Finally, they made it to the hospital exit without seeing the man again. Ian pulled her aside. "He'll be watching the exits."

"He can't watch them all without help. If he isn't working alone, others could be watching all the exits." Jonna wished they could grab some nursing garb. A man holding flowers walked with a nurse pushing a woman in a wheelchair. "I have an idea."

She headed down the hallway in search of the gift store. Inside they found ball caps and hoodies. "We can change into these and maybe throw them off."

"Not for long."

"We don't need long." She selected a cap and a hoodie for herself. Tossed Ian the right size. "We can pretend to be a couple—that'll add another layer to our cover."

Ian's cheek hitched up. "Good idea. That will buy us five minutes."

"We should ditch the rental car too."

"Nah. They waited for us to show up at Uncle Gil's room. They probably don't know what vehicle we arrived in. We can still safely leave in that."

And go where? Doubts crawled over her. Maybe she shouldn't have come back.

She shook the second-guessing off. They were here. She would finish it. One way or another. She found a bouquet of balloons filled with helium. That could help with their disguise.

After making their purchases, they donned the caps and hoodies in the store then left. Ian pulled her close. Holding the bouquet of balloons, they exited the hospital along with a family as though they were with the group.

Ian tugged her closer. Veered right away from the family. His arm around her, he sunk his head low, near hers. "What are you doing?" she whispered.

"Going along with your disguise. This was your idea, remember? We're a couple."

"Yeah, but you don't have to walk so close."

His proximity made her dizzy and she needed to focus. She wasn't sure they could make it through this together.

But she was certain they wouldn't make it through apart.

A balloon popped, startling her. Concrete splintered next to her head. She instinctively ducked.

"Get down!" Ian pushed her to the ground with him. "Let go of the balloons. They'll give us away now."

If they were taking shots at her in public, the modus operandi had just shifted.

EIGHTEEN

Ian shielded Jonna with his own body. Only one shot had been taken. No one had screamed or reacted.

Ian hadn't heard gunfire. He'd only heard the balloon pop. Had the popping masked the sound? Or had it been a sniper shooting from a distance?

He calculated the general trajectory. "I think it was a sniper. Maybe he's in that building over there." Or if he was former military, he could be a mile or more away.

Not good.

The sniper was either waiting for them to make a move that would put Jonna back into the path of a bullet, or he was on the move to come closer to them himself.

"Come on, let's go," he said. "We have to get out of here."

"There could be more than one gunman."

"That's another reason why we have to get out of here," he said. "Stick close to me. And use the cars as cover as much as possible. Let's keep our conversation to a minimum and our voices down. We don't know how many are hunting for us."

Jonna wasn't a rookie, and probably didn't need his reminders. From behind the concrete pillar, he crawled into the parking lot between two minivans. They could get lost in this parking lot. Escape that way.

A few passersby gave them odd looks. Ian waved them away. He didn't want their stares or questions to telepath their location to the sniper, or worse, to put innocent bystanders in danger.

Ducking, he continued using vehicles as cover and Jonna followed.

"Where are we going?" she whispered.

"To the other side of the hospital." He hoped another sniper wasn't waiting there. "We can grab a cab."

"You want me to call for one?"

"I don't think we have time to wait."

Glass shattered in the vehicle near them. He covered Jonna again.

"I see your point. So we're going to take someone else's cab."

"Got a better idea?" He slowly eased away from her, but not too far.

"Let's go after the sniper. Get him to talk."

Her words startled him, but they probably shouldn't have. He couldn't help but grin as he studied her. "You're serious."

"Better than running. I didn't come here to run."

"But you expect me to protect you. And that means letting me decide which option is safe." He shared a good, long look, her brown eyes taking him in. This wasn't the time to get lost in them.

"We can do this. All you have to do is watch my back. Maybe we can't get to the sniper, but we could still try to ambush the guy who stalked us in the hospital."

He nodded. "Come on, then."

Hiding behind cars and between palm trees, they

made their way around the hospital complex, watching for the man inside. He had to come out at some point unless they'd missed him, or he was using another exit.

Minutes ticked by. Ian started to believe this wasn't going to work. But he'd have to convince Jonna.

"Look, we're too exposed. Let's go somewhere and regroup. We could get ambushed ourselves. At least we tried. We just missed our opportunity. Waiting for him isn't worth your life." He tugged her closer. "And now we need new disguises."

She angled away from him. "We're no longer a couple. Does that work?"

Regrettably, yes. They hurried around the west side of the hospital complex, passing garbage and hazardous waste receptacles. Near the corner of the building, Ian hesitated. "Wait. Let me look."

Ian edged to the corner and peered around. Cars waited under the drop-off circle. No taxis. How did he get her out of here? Maybe they should call a cab after all.

"Ian," she whispered and tugged on his sleeve. "Footfalls. Someone's coming around the building."

Could be anyone. Danger felt like it closed in on them from all sides. Ian had been an idiot to agree to this. "Get behind me."

A man rounded the corner. Their hospital stalker. Ian punched him in the face. He slammed against the wall. Jonna twisted his arm around. The man grimaced in pain but made no attempt to fight back.

He actually had the nerve to laugh. "You don't have a weapon."

"Neither do you," she said.

"I don't need one. I'm not going to hurt you. I just want to talk. I'm…MDPD PCS."

"Miami-Dade Police. Public Corruption Section." Jonna translated. "Doesn't mean we can trust you."

"Look. I don't know who to trust either, except for you. Can we at least go somewhere to talk?"

"How'd you know we would be here?"

"I didn't know for sure. But I knew Gil Reeves had been taken here. I was the one to find him. I'm Detective Mason Claiborne."

"Why did you chase us in the hospital?"

"I wasn't chasing you. I needed to talk, and didn't want to lose you after I'd found you. I figured Jonna would go under the radar and back into hiding. I should have introduced myself on the elevator but didn't want to draw any attention to you when there were other people around. I admit, I could have handled that better."

Ian wasn't sure what to think, but felt they needed to hear the man out. Jonna gave him a subtle nod. She agreed as though she'd heard his thoughts.

"There's a sniper who's already taken a shot at her. I'm not sure, but I think it came from the bank building across the street," Ian said. "Can you get us out of here?"

Jonna slowly released the detective.

Claiborne shook his arms out, and arched a brow as though afraid Jonna would hurt him again. Ian held back a grin.

"I can try." He adjusted his jacket. "You wait inside. I'll grab my car and pull around to the emergency entrance and pick you up there. If someone's watching, we'll have to lose them."

"It's the best we've got," Ian said.

He waited with Jonna inside the emergency room entrance. Claiborne would text Ian when he'd pulled the car around. But fifteen minutes had already gone by.

"What do you think is keeping him?" Jonna paced in the small corner where they waited.

"I don't even know if we can trust him," Ian said.

Jonna pulled her hood back over her head as if preparing to make another run for it. Claiborne had to be there soon.

Finally, Ian's cell buzzed. He read the message. "Show time."

Jonna sat in the back of the midsize sedan with darkened windows while Claiborne stopped at their rental to retrieve their weapons. She hunkered low in the seat, in case they'd been made and someone else tried to take a shot. Her life had completely spun out of control.

Ian sat in the front with Claiborne. On the off chance that the detective wasn't aboveboard, Ian could potentially protect them. But going with the man was taking a big leap of faith. He could be playing them.

On her smartphone, she looked up everything she could about Detective Mason Claiborne. The man in the driver's seat matched the images she found online, so it seemed he really was a cop, as he had claimed. But that didn't mean she could fully buy his story. Given that the mayor was a potential suspect, she couldn't seriously trust anything she might have learned about Claiborne.

She watched the roads. Hoped Ian paid attention to any tails. "Where are you taking us?"

"I know a place. It's safe."

Yeah, it could be a setup.

"No," Ian said.

"Where would you like to go?" Claiborne slowed at a stoplight.

"Somewhere public," Jonna said. "If we've been followed or someone shows up there, we'll know we can't trust you."

Still waiting at the light, the man lifted his palms. "If someone follows us there, I have nothing to do with that."

"Then make sure we're not followed," Ian said.

Jonna and Ian tracked so well together.

She allowed herself a moment to take in the sights. The palm trees—something not seen in Washington State. Even in the middle of the winter, the temperature here was seventy.

But…she was in Miami. Fleeing for her life. Trying to find who was behind this.

Surreal. Completely surreal.

She closed her eyes and wished for her relaxing home on the coast and the sound of waves crashing in a Pacific-brewed storm. And Ian—she wished he could be there too, but she ran from that thought. Hard and fast, she ran. She couldn't let him in. Not too close.

Claiborne had a distinct northeastern accent. But then again, Miami brimmed with transplants from all over. "You're not from around here, are you?"

"I was with the NYPD for ten years. Wife's parents retired here. They had her late in life. She wanted to be closer, so here we are. My first year, the humidity almost killed me." Claiborne pulled into the parking lot at a Denny's restaurant. "Here, this public enough for you?"

"It'll do." Ian shifted to look at the man.

The detective made to open his door.

"Wait. Let's talk here. This is too sensitive to talk about in public." Jonna sat up and peered around them.

The streets were busy, bustling with life—people and cars. Miami, just how she remembered it.

A place to hide—whether you were the hunter or the hunted. She couldn't calm her heart. Not as long as she was here and this wasn't over.

"Tell us what you know," Ian said.

"I had an informant who was killed three years ago. You might know him. Derrick Thompson."

Her informant… Jonna's pulse inched up, but she committed to nothing. "Keep talking."

"He had a wife and three kids. Did you know that?"

Was that true? Jonna hadn't known. Guilt suffused her.

"Young boys that'll grow into teenagers. Hard to handle at that age alone. I keep tabs on them. Maybe I help out a little at times. Just said to his wife that we'd been friends. She might blame me for his death if she knew he'd been keeping me informed. But about two weeks ago she called me to say she doesn't want me to come around to see the boys anymore. I can tell something has her spooked."

If Claiborne was this altruistic, maybe they could trust him.

"What do you think scared her?" Ian asked.

"She knows something, that's what. Or maybe someone just thinks she does. So I waited in the shadows. I watched her house."

Tension ignited in Jonna's shoulders as Claiborne dragged his story out.

"One night, a guy shows up there. He's in and out real quick. I get that gut feeling that I need to follow him. So I did. He went to a few bars and hopped around town, probably trying to shake any tails. Guess where he ends up?"

"I have no idea." But she thought she just might.

"Talking to another guy who works for none other than Mayor Hendrix."

NINETEEN

Jonna said nothing to the man's comment about the mayor. Interesting. Ian assumed she wasn't going to share her information until she'd heard everything.

And Ian had thought he couldn't admire her more than he already did.

Ian realized he should call his uncle to verify this guy. Uncle Gil had said he didn't know whom to trust.

Hand pressed against the nine-millimeter Glock resting on his thigh, Ian continued to watch out the vehicle windows as he listened to the detective. Was this guy giving them an especially long spiel so they could be followed and ambushed here? Had someone been tracking his phone? Ian didn't think so. His detailed account sounded legit. Still, Ian would remain vigilant.

Having his weapon to protect them had been worth the risk of retrieving it.

"We're listening," Ian said. "Keep talking. We need to speed up this conversation so we can get moving. I don't like sitting in one spot too long."

"I hear you. So I got closer to this guy, hoping to find out more about the mayor. Danny is his name."

Surprised to hear that name, Ian arched a brow. Was

it the same Danny that had shown up in Washington? The detective misunderstood Ian's reaction.

"Hey, I'm good at what I do," Claiborne said. "I know how to get people to talk. It's why I'm in the public corruption department."

He angled toward the back seat and looked at Jonna. "The guy's cell rings and he answers. I heard him say something about, 'that pig, that woman cop, Detective Strand.'"

Jonna leaned forward. "In what context?"

"This is where I lost track of him. Like he just disappeared off the planet."

"Because he came to Washington," she said. "His name was Danny Johnson. He shot me and left me for dead three years ago here in Florida. Then he tracked me to an obscure location in Washington and tried to kill me again."

Claiborne frowned. "I'm sorry about that. I noticed you said, 'His name was,' as in past tense."

"Because he's dead now," she said.

"None of your story explains how you knew anything about what was going on," Ian interrupted. "How did you find Gil? How did you know Jonna would show up at the hospital?"

The detective pinched his nose, then dropped it, exhaustion showing in the creases on his forty-something face. "I'm good at math."

"Huh?"

"I can put two and two together." He snorted. "That, and my wife, Nadine, is Gil's assistant. You called her, remember? Said you were worried about him."

"Nadine is your wife?"

"That she is. Gil was in a coma. I hear he woke up.

Probably doesn't know it was me who found him. See, my wife also happened to know about you, Mr. Brady. Maybe she shouldn't have shared so much with me, but things being what they are, and some serious corruption going on out there, I decided to butt my nose into this. Besides, you're linked to my investigation."

"Let's drive. Go to that safe house you mentioned," Jonna said. "You can tell us about your investigation on the way."

"You got it." He put the car back into gear. "I've been working on gathering evidence on a private vendor that works with the county. Tried to cheat the city. We got him in interrogation and he wanted to cut a deal, brought up the mayor. I didn't believe it. Why should I?"

"But you didn't dismiss it either, did you?" Jonna asked from the back seat.

"No. If I've learned one thing in all my years as a detective, it's never leave a stone unturned."

"Sounds like we need to pay the mayor a visit," Ian said.

Claiborne narrowed his eyes as he turned down another road, steering through a classy neighborhood. "That's not going to be easy."

"I have a connection," Ian said. "A friend in the DSS. I need to give him a call anyway. He could help. We can trust him."

"What's your plan? What are you thinking? We might be thinking the same thing." The detective turned down a long-winding drive.

"What I hope you're *both* thinking is that I need to confront the mayor," Jonna said. "Just me and him. Maybe seeing me face-to-face will surprise him enough that I can get him talking. Get a confession."

Claiborne laughed.

Ian eyed the lavish house they'd parked in front of. "Whose home is this?"

"An old friend. I put away a guy who embezzled a hundred thousand dollars from her. Even got the money back. She offered the house if we ever needed it. She's traveling abroad for a couple of weeks. Oh…" Claiborne smiled. "And you're going to love this part. It's a couple of blocks from the mayor's house."

"What?" What was this guy trying to pull?

"I like it," Jonna said. "Nobody will look for me so close to him."

"See, I told you we were thinking alike."

And the closer she was to the mayor—the sooner she could get this over with and get back to her life—the better.

Claiborne led them into the house. Mahogany doors. Shiny dark wood floors.

Jonna was afraid to touch anything. Walking by the polished-to-perfection traditional furniture, the curio cabinet brimming with crystal and porcelain figurines, reminded her of going to those fancy stores with Mom before she died. Jonna could hear Mom's voice in her head. "Don't touch anything. If you break it then we'll have to pay for it."

Unfortunately, there had been one time when her younger sister Sadie knocked a small cup over and it shattered. Though that wasn't the best memory, thoughts of her family made her heart warm. At least she still had close relationships with her siblings—Sadie and Cora— and her aunt Debby. Quinn—she'd have to make an effort to find and contact him once this was over. In the meantime, she'd let her aunt know she would be taking a short trip, and had been cryptic. She hadn't wanted the woman to worry about her. Still, a shard of guilt jabbed her heart.

They continued down the hallway into the kitchen. Shiny copper pans hung from hooks secured to the ceiling. *Wow.* She would love to have a kitchen like this at her lodge.

They settled at the table. Claiborne pulled open the large, expensive refrigerator. "It's stocked. Make yourself at home. Would you like sodas—there are five different kinds in here—and juice, milk or fancy water?"

"Are you positive this is okay with the owner? And that it's safe?" Ian asked.

He ran a hand through his hair, clearly nervous about any place he hadn't already checked out and secured ahead of time. That endeared him to her in a thousand ways it shouldn't.

Of course, she knew he was only doing his job—the one she hadn't made easy for him by coming here.

Detective Claiborne set a couple of Cokes on the table since they hadn't shared their requests. Decisive. She liked that about him. "Look, I understand you have trust issues. Call my wife, Nadine. Call your uncle. I'm sure he'll vouch for me. But right now, we're wasting time. Now, either you're in or you're out—and if you're out then you'll have to find your own safe house."

Jonna pressed her hand on Ian's arm, and he stopped pacing. "We're in." She gazed into Ian's turbulent blue eyes. "Call your friend with the DSS. See what he can do for us. I need a way in to face the mayor. To surprise him. Maybe I can record the conversation somehow."

Detective Claiborne grabbed a seat. "Mayor Hendrix has a big charity in his name."

He took a swig of his soda and watched them over the rim. Studying their reaction?

"Wait. You're not saying it's a money-laundering scheme, are you?" Maybe that's where the money trail had been all along.

"Tomorrow." Claiborne had finished his soda. "We can make definitive plans tomorrow. Tonight you sleep. And I'm going to call Nadine. She'll bring us some pizza for later."

"Oh that's not necessary," Jonna said.

"I'm not doing it for you." The detective tossed his can into the recycling bin. "I have every intention of hanging out here with you two. Staying the night. Gil would have my hide if I didn't keep you safe. That, and I want to eat pizza and see my wife."

"Well, at least you're honest," Ian said. "I like that about you, Claiborne."

He showed them the alarm system. "You don't want to make a mistake with this alarm, believe you me. The cops will be here and you'll have to explain what you're doing here when you've never even met the owner. Besides, then your safe house is blown, *capisce*?"

"Capisce." Jonna said as she moseyed down the hallway. After choosing a bedroom and tossing her duffel bag on the bed, Jonna washed her face and freshened up in the bathroom. She felt uncomfortable and out of place in this home. But she focused on the task ahead of her.

Crossing her arms, she looked out the window at the landscaped yard and the palms, feeling the time difference to her bones.

A soft knock came at the door. "Come in. It's not locked."

Ian approached from behind. "How are you doing?"

"I wish I could go outside and walk around, but that might not be the best idea."

"Right. Someone could see you, especially since we're so close to our target." Concern edged his tone. "Jonna, are you sure about this?"

"No, I'm not." She could be about to walk into a trap. She could end up dead. "But I was minding my own business. They came after me, remember? They started it, and I'm going to finish it." Tough words, those. Could she really go through with this?

She turned then and found him closer than she'd expected. Jonna gazed up into his striking blues. She wanted to get lost in them. Except this wasn't the time to get slammed with thoughts of being in Ian's arms. With dreams of kissing a man she could never be with. "Did you call your friend?"

A storm approached in his eyes. "I left him a message and said it was urgent. He'll get back to me soon." Ian took a step closer and blocked her escape with his muscular form and broad shoulders. Her breath caught.

His musky scent wrapped around her. Jonna tried to hold his gaze, even though she wanted to run away.

He lifted both hands and cupped her cheeks, slid his hands into her hair and leaned closer. "I don't want you to get hurt. This isn't how I would ever protect someone. Especially someone I care about."

She understood this went far beyond any typical protection detail for him and that's what made it more dangerous for the both of them. *You shouldn't care about*

me, Ian. Not like that. And I shouldn't care about you.
But she wouldn't say those words out loud. Not now.

Her eyes burned. How did his nearness stir her emotions like this? She absolutely couldn't get all sentimental on him. That wasn't her way. But apparently it was when it came to Ian Brady. "I know I'm asking too much of you," she said.

"I'm prepared to give my life." Tenderness flashed in the midst of the tempest in his gaze.

Her heart couldn't take much more. She hated that she was putting him in the line of fire.

"Promise me you won't do anything impulsive," he said. "Let's make solid plans and then we have to agree on them or it's a no go."

When she didn't answer he dropped his hands to her shoulders and gripped. "Jonna. Promise me."

"I never make promises."

TWENTY

Ian wanted to squeeze her. To shake some sense into her. This is exactly what Uncle Gil had warned him about.

"Ian, it's not like the police aren't involved in this. Detective Claiborne will help us make plans and maybe your friend too. I don't think we can go in fully sanctioned. If there is law enforcement on the trafficking ring's payroll, getting that sanctioned go-ahead could cost our lives. You know that."

Indeed, he did.

The sudden desire to kiss her long and thoroughly entered his mind unbidden. He dropped his hands from her shoulders. She appeared relieved. Standing so close to Jonna messed with his mind and heart.

The inky blackness of the window caught his attention. "You shouldn't stand there. Someone could see inside."

She moved and he twisted the mini blinds and secured the drapes. "Doesn't look like anyone has actually used these in a while."

"I think they're mostly for decoration," she said. "Not to actually cover the window."

"Hey, guys, pizza's here. And I want you to meet Nadine." Claiborne's voice boomed down the hallway.

"You go on. I need to call someone." Ian stared at his phone. It showed that he had a voicemail. "Looks like a call came in but I didn't hear it."

Jonna nodded and moved past him, then paused. "Ian, for your sake I wish you weren't involved in this, but for my sake I'm glad that you are. Like I said before, I trust you."

He followed her out of her room, then went to the room he'd chosen for himself and shut the door. Closed the mini blinds as well. He'd given all the doors and windows a look to make sure all was locked up. Checked their potential exits in case of trouble. As long as no one knew they were here, this was as safe as they could get.

He listened to the voicemail, then returned Patrick's call, hoping he'd get the guy this time.

"Ian!"

"Hey there."

"I thought we'd never connect. I've been trying to reach you for days. I've been worried."

"I know. Sorry about that, but a lot's happened over the past few days." Ian went ahead and told Patrick everything. "And now, we're here in Miami, camped in the same neighborhood as the mayor's house."

Ian blew out a breath. Telling the story, laying it all out there for Patrick, stirred doubt in his gut.

"I need you to listen to me, Ian. The reason I called you was that we wanted to bring on an independent investigator to keep tabs on Miami's mayor."

"Say what?"

"That's right. I knew your uncle lived there, so I thought you could visit him and on the side work for us freelance. Nobody blames you for what happened here, even though you blame yourself."

"Why is the DSS investigating the mayor?"

Patrick blew out a breath. "This goes no further than you, right?"

"Understood."

"We have a visiting foreign dignitary coming to Miami. He has connections to the mayor. Those connections might not be aboveboard."

"Jonna and Claiborne think Mayor Hendrix could be linked to the human-trafficking ring supposedly dismantled three years ago. There was a money trail they never found. Maybe he's laundering money through his charity. Are other law-enforcement agencies involved?"

"We're holding this close to the chest since we suspect someone could be tipping him off. Someone on the inside. That's why I wanted to bring you on to work independently while visiting your uncle."

"Jonna plans to face the mayor. Go in wired and get him talking. Any chance you can help with that so we can knock this out before it gets messy?"

"No chance. That can't happen, Ian. Get her out of there. She could blow this all out of the water and jeopardize lives."

"I hear you. But she's determined. They came after her, and she wants to end this. I'm not sure what I can do to stop her."

"How about reason with her? But do not tell her anything I've told you. It could threaten everything if not cost me my job. There's more going on that I haven't told you."

"It would help if I could tell her it will end soon. Is anyone going to arrest the mayor?"

"I can't tell you that, or give you an end date."

"Okay. You've given me a lot to think about. I'll call you back with an update."

"You got it."

Ian made to end the call.

"Ian…"

"I'm here."

"I'll let you know if something changes. Maybe the powers that be will want her to go in after all, but we would be there to protect her. But as things stand, do not let her face Mayor Hendrix."

"I understand."

He hung up. And like Jonna, he could make no promises.

They finished up the pizza Nadine had brought. She ate with them. "Gil is doing better," she reported. "He still has two officers posted by his door and was resting when I went to see him this afternoon."

"I say we sleep on it, then tomorrow we put our heads together." Claiborne boxed up the leftovers.

Jonna frowned. "I don't think I'm going to sleep tonight. Why not start talking about plans right now? That would give us the rest of the night to think on them."

The detective arched a brow. "I know what you want to do, but you can't just march into his house, all wired up, and get him to talk."

"Don't insult my intelligence." Jonna injected a teasing tone, but she was also dead serious.

Nadine averted her gaze and busied herself cleaning up after them.

"You don't need to do that," Jonna said. "We can clean up after ourselves."

"I need to keep busy and you need to talk this out." Nadine smiled and continued removing the paper plates. Sweet woman but also no-nonsense.

Jonna desperately wanted to know what Ian was thinking, as long as his ideas weren't going to nix her plans. She was counting on him to be all the way in with her.

Ian pushed from the wall where he leaned. "I heard from my buddy in the DSS. He's going to get back to me tomorrow, so we wait. We shouldn't make plans or any moves until I hear back. In the meantime, we can look into the charity. Follow other leads as long as that doesn't include leaving this house."

Right. Finding more evidence could only be a good thing, but still, Jonna wasn't going to wait forever. "The whole point in this is the element of surprise. The longer I'm here, the better chance the mayor, or whoever else is involved, will have time to prepare."

"You're forgetting something," Claiborne said. "Someone shot at you at the hospital. They already know you're here."

"But the mayor can't know I'm coming for him, specifically."

"Why does it have to be you who confronts him?" Ian asked. "There are any number of others who could face him and ask the hard questions."

Jonna's throat tightened. She fisted her hands. "The whole reason I came to Miami was to face him and end this. What are you doing, Ian?"

He pursed his lips and leveled his gaze at her. "You said you trusted me to protect you. I need you to trust me now, when I say it's best if you don't go in to face him just yet. At the very least, we should wait to hear back from my contact."

"If it were up to you, you'd have us get back on a plane tonight and head to a safe house somewhere in another state. Am I wrong?"

Ian glanced at Detective Claiborne and Nadine, who stared at them wide-eyed as if they were watching a lover's quarrel.

"If you guys will excuse me, I need to talk to Jonna alone."

Ian gently grabbed her elbow and urged her out of the kitchen. Jonna wasn't sure she wanted to go, but she'd give him the benefit of a doubt. There could be something he didn't want to say in front of Claiborne and his wife.

"What are you doing?" Her whisper was forceful as he guided her down the hallway of the luxurious home.

He ushered her into the room where she'd planned to stay tonight if she could actually sleep.

"Jonna, you said you trusted me. Is that true or not?"

"It's true. To a point. Are you going to tell me what's going on?"

"I have new information but I'm not at liberty to share it, all right?" His expression suddenly turned soft, his next words tender. "Please, I'm begging you—just hold off for now. It isn't all on you."

The tenderness in his expression and tone could turn her to mush when she was trying to be strong. More than anything she wanted him to kiss her, but a more completely foolish thought she'd never had. She sagged and slumped against the wall.

"I set my mind on something and I'm like a bulldog." Then she realized he had a way with those attack animals, just the same as he had a way with her. Was that such a bad thing?

"If there's one thing I've learned about you it's that you're determined and strong."

"Something else I hope you've learned is that I trust you, Ian. And I'm going to keep trusting you. Maybe I coerced you into coming down here against your better judgement, but now that we're here, I'm going to follow your lead. We'll wait. I'll give you a day. You have tomorrow, and then we'll make our plans unless you can give me some new information that changes the game."

"Fair enough."

Jonna offered him a small grin. How could she not? "Now, if you'll excuse me, since we're not strategizing, I'm beyond exhausted. I think I'll sleep while I can."

He headed for the door.

"Ian, wait."

He paused but didn't turn.

"You probably plan to stay up and remain on guard and protect me, but that's not necessary. Nobody knows we're here. Detective Claiborne and his wife are here too. Take this chance to get some rest for once in your life. You look awful."

Turning, he eyed her and laughed. "Thanks."

"You're welcome."

She watched him leave, then shut the door. Jonna fell onto the bed, afraid to sleep, but she couldn't remember ever being this exhausted. Fear twisted with apprehension over what she might face in the next few hours and days. But what right did she have to fear what was coming? Hadn't she brought this on herself?

No. She hadn't. She'd walked away from this kind of danger, only to have it follow her. In the darkness, lightning flashed, then a roll of thunder.

She closed her eyes as rain pounded outside. Maybe,

just maybe, she could fall asleep if she let herself pretend she was back in her cabin on the Washington coast and all was well with her life.

She could also pretend that Ian Brady hadn't found a way through her barricade and into her heart.

A sound startled Jonna awake. What was it? She sat up in the dark and looked around. Her smartphone glowed. A text?

"What?" She mumbled and rubbed her eyes. Who would be sending a text this time of night? She blinked the blurriness away and read the text from Aunt Debby.

Her heart hammered at the next words.

We have your aunt. Come out of the house alone. Be at the corner within the next sixty seconds or we will kill her. Tell no one or we will kill her.

We. Will. Kill. Her.

TWENTY-ONE

Shock shoved her over.

Sixty seconds!

No time to get her brain in gear. It had taken her ten to read and comprehend the message. She had no time to spare for anything, not even thinking. And that was their strategy. Jonna sat up.

Where am I? Whose room is this?

Panic paralyzed her, then realization dawned. A safe house. But not so safe after all, since it seemed they knew she was here.

Jeans. Where were her jeans?

Where did I put my clothes?

Forty-five seconds...

She searched the room and found her duffel bag. Dumped clothes onto the bed. She couldn't get dressed fast enough. Grabbed some sweats. What did she care what she wore? Aunt Debby's life was in jeopardy.

She had no doubt they had her aunt—the call came from Aunt Debby's cell. Maybe that could be faked but she couldn't count on it just being a bluff.

Jonna tried to pull the sweats on, then realized she already had her jeans on. She'd fallen asleep in her clothes. But shoes. She needed shoes.

Thirty seconds...

She must have kicked her shoes off in her sleep. She dropped to her knees and reached under the bed, where she found them. Then slipped them on. No time to tie the laces. She grabbed her gun and her cell.

And quietly opened the door.

Slipped down the hallway.

Oh, God, please let Ian not be awake. Please don't let him stop me...

What was she praying?

Oh, God, please let Ian follow me and get us out of this.

And faced the alarm system.

What was the code? What was the code? She cleared her mind—this was life or death—and pictured the numbers Claiborne had said.

As soon as she pressed the numbers, someone could hear the small beeps. She focused on the door. She'd have to turn off the alarm, unlock the door and hope no one saw her.

Fifteen seconds...

She entered the number and ran for the door, unlocking the dead bolt.

"Where do you think you're going?"

Ian.

She squeezed her eyes shut.

"I have less time than I need to get to the corner or they are going to kill my Aunt Debby."

"I can't let you go out there."

Jonna whirled around to face Ian and aimed her gun at him.

He threw his hands up, shock and anger apparent in his features.

"You're not going to stop me." She backed away from him and out the door. Saw him calculating the risk of trying to get in her way.

Oh, God, what do I do? I have no choices!

"Jonna, please, let me help you." Desperation flooded his voice. Hurt and anger flickered in his gaze.

Jonna had to save her aunt. She couldn't care about what Ian needed. "I'm not supposed to tell anyone. They'll kill her if they even suspect I've told you. You have to stay here—and let me go. Then find us, Ian. Save Aunt Debby."

And me... But she wouldn't get her hopes up.

Jonna slipped out the door and out into the night, a light mist falling as the storm moved through. She made her way quietly around the palms, jogging down the driveway and onto the sidewalk. They said the corner. Be at the corner. She'd head for the closest corner, hope it was the right one.

She had lost track of time, but had done the best she could do. *God, please save my aunt. She had nothing at all to do with this.*

Jonna continued to jog, the corner in sight. But no one else was out at two in the morning. She heard the slow rumble of a vehicle approaching from behind.

Her heart hammered. Palms slicked, she gripped the weapon. Why had she brought it? Using it would only get Aunt Debby killed. They would strip her of the gun anyway. Her cell phone too.

Unless…unless she found another way. If she hid her phone long enough then dropped it in the vehicle, that would give Ian a chance to track her.

The vehicle sped up. Jonna tensed, prepared to use the weapon. She turned to face a big black Suburban. Lights flashed in her eyes. She held her weapon behind her back.

What am I doing? What am I doing?

But these men, this man running things, knew her weakness. Her aunt Debby. She'd do anything to save her aunt. Including give herself up without a struggle.

And that's exactly what she did.

Two masked men dressed in black jumped from the SUV. Jonna resisted the urge to fight.

"Where's my aunt? Release her and I'll go with you." Neither replied.

One man grabbed her while another put a black bag over her head, removed her gun, secured her hands and quickly loaded her in the SUV.

She tried to gasp for breath. Couldn't breathe.

Oh, God, help me...

"I want to see my aunt." Jonna sat in what seemed to be a basement with the bag still over her head. The basement was dark. It was certainly cold.

Oh Lord, please help me. What have I done?

But she'd had no choice. None whatsoever if it meant saving her aunt. Tears burned behind her eyes, but she fought them. Sucked in a breath. She had to be strong. There might still be a way out of this.

Please protect my aunt...

"Why are you doing this?" she asked, but no one answered her. She sensed no one was in the basement with her. How long would they keep her? How long would it take for Ian to discover her?

Heavy footfalls—more than one person—descended

the steps into the basement. Through the bag's thin material she detected lights had been turned on.

Would Mayor Hendrix confront her down here? Find out what information she had and who she'd told before he had her killed?

"I did what you asked, now where is my aunt?"

Someone drew a long breath, then, "You're not in any position to make demands, but I'm not someone to go back on my word. Your aunt will be released at the end of our interview."

The voice. Whose voice was that? It sounded familiar. "Hendrix? Is that you?"

The bag came off her head. She squinted when bright lights flashed. Finally, her eyes adjusted.

It really was Mayor Hendrix. She would get to face off with him after all, but she was the one at a disadvantage. And she had no way to record the conversation. She wasn't wired to those who could listen.

His gaze filled with regret, his frown one of deep sadness, he said, "I'm sorry about all of this, Jonna."

Funny. She didn't believe him.

"Please tell me what you know," he said.

So he could kill the others involved? The detective and his wife, Ian, Gil? She'd leave all of them out of it if she could, but the mayor obviously knew. Gil had already been beaten. Hendrix had also known about the safe house. "Tell me where my aunt is. Prove she's okay, and I'll tell you what I know."

"I've already told you she'll be released unharmed if you cooperate. You'll have to trust me."

Trust him? How could he ask that of her?

Uncertainty skirted across his gaze. Right. He couldn't even trust the outcome of his own operation.

Still, antagonizing him would get her nowhere. She would cooperate if there was a chance it would save her aunt. She would also cooperate to buy time and pray Ian found her.

"Okay, I'll trust that you are a man of your word. I don't know much. If you had left me where I was in Washington, you would have been better off. I've spent the past few years trying to forget everything I left behind here. But then your sending someone there to finish the job and kill me only made me want to find out why. I didn't even know who wanted me dead."

"And what did you find out?" he asked.

"Three years ago, I only knew that there was a money trail. A shell company. But we hit a brick wall trying to connect it to anyone. It wasn't until the man you sent after me in Washington was hit by a car that I realized you might be connected. He said your name just before he died. That's all I know."

Mayor Hendrix telegraphed that someone stood behind her. Someone he feared. What was going on?

That someone stepped into her line of vision. Senator Shelby?

"Unfortunately I believe you, Jonna. If you knew more, then we wouldn't be talking in this manner. I would be accused and maybe charged, though I'd never be convicted. I'll tell you the pieces you missed before you die. You deserve that. Your aunt will be released. No sense in stirring the cauldron further, considering the thugs who already made a mess. They'll be blamed, and misdirection will take investigators far from me or my foster brother, Mayor Hendrix."

Surprise rolled through her.

He smiled. "That's right. Didn't you read my story? I

was an orphan. Grew up as a foster kid. Made my way up through the ranks to become a senator. That rarely happens. I started out with a disadvantage—no family connections or patronage to help smooth my way. So I became industrious and masterminded a human-trafficking ring. The money is laundered through the mayor's charity for needy children."

"You make me sick. Both of you." Jonna wanted to spit.

"It's not by choice," the mayor said. "Please believe me."

"Oh, he's telling the truth," the senator admitted, sounding bored. "He didn't want to be involved. But I hold something over him—pictures that would destroy his career. With the laundering system arranged, everything could have kept going, even after you shut down the trafficking ring. Another operation is always waiting to take its place."

"I was the one to pressure the feds and cops to shut down the ring, Jonna," Mayor Hendrix said. "I knew if the investigation continued, eventually my charity would be discovered as being involved. Anyone who found out would have to be eliminated—more lives lost. I'm so sorry about all of this."

In his voice, she heard the truth. But the man wasn't strong enough to let the truth come out. He couldn't risk losing everything because of what he and his foster brother had done.

Against the wall, she spotted two men—the attackers from Washington. They looked eager to hurt her; after all, they probably blamed her for Danny's death.

"I don't get it. Why did my name come up again? Why did you look for me and bring me back into this?"

Senator Shelby crossed his arms. "I'm running for re-election in a nasty race. My opponent is digging for dirt wherever he can find it. All loose ends need to be tied. One of the jerks got jealous of Danny and told me that you were still alive. So I sent them to take care of you. Once you showed up here, I suspected you must know something and that you'd come to confront me. But... I was wrong."

Except now she knew everything. Now she was going to die.

TWENTY-TWO

Ian aimed his weapon, having put down his phone after recording the entire conversation. He'd made his way through the few men who had been in the home as a security detail. The detective had secured Jonna's aunt Debby in a bedroom upstairs. Ian knew all the tricks of the security-detail trade. He had incapacitated each one of them one at a time.

Now to get Jonna out of the basement alive.

Since the senator had confessed all, she had few short minutes. Ian recognized the two men against the wall and they would likely do the dirty deed. Certainly not the senator or the mayor. It wasn't likely either of the two politicians even carried a weapon. That's why they had hired guns.

Ian aimed his weapon, calculating who to take out first. And when to do it. He wasn't law enforcement, but he would protect Jonna.

To Ian's shock, the mayor slipped a gun out from under his jacket.

Sweat beaded his temples as Ian fingered the trigger.

Mayor Hendrix pointed the weapon at the senator, his next words directed at his foster brother. "I can't let this go any further. I'm going to own up to my part in it, and admit that I succumbed to your blackmail. I can't knowingly stand by and let you murder someone right in front of me. I turned a blind eye for far too long on the trafficking ring. This ends here. Tonight."

"You're right," Senator Shelby said, gesturing to his henchmen. "It does."

Ian made his presence known, aiming his Glock at the thugs who drew their guns. "Mayor Hendrix, these men were going to kill you. Keep your gun trained on the senator. Help is on the way. Now, you two, drop your weapons," Ian said to the men he'd already faced in Washington.

Backing up, he positioned himself between Jonna and the men. He couldn't allow her to get caught in the crossfire.

In his peripheral vision, Ian could see the mayor's wide eyes and the nervous tick in his cheek, the trembling hands. He didn't appear to be the kind of man who was comfortable wielding deadly firearms.

The senator revealed his own weapon and gunfire resounded as time slowed. Ian covered Jonna with his body as he traded shots with the thugs, who took cover against the wall. The mayor dropped to the ground. The senator as well.

Footfalls resounded on the steps. "Police! Drop your weapons!"

Ian immediately put his Glock down. More gunfire resumed. He shielded Jonna and cut her hand ties; they slipped to the floor where he protected her body with his own. Finally, the room fell quiet.

"You all right?" Claiborne grabbed Ian's arm to pull him up.

"I think so." Ian sat up and tugged Jonna into a sitting position, his focus on her and nothing else that happened around them. "Are you hurt?"

She shook her head. "My aunt?"

Claiborne crouched down to eye level. "We have her. She's fine. A little groggy, but she'll be okay. She's with Nadine."

Ian stood with Claiborne and helped Jonna to her feet.

Her brown eyes took him in, emotion he couldn't define brimming in her gaze. "Thank you. I knew you would find us and protect us."

"I might have been too late, Jonna, if I hadn't seen you leaving. Why didn't you come to me first?"

"They didn't give me any time. Besides…I was sure you would come through. You could find me with the tracker app on my phone. I dropped it into the vehicle."

"They must have found and destroyed it. It didn't work."

"What? Then, how did you find me?"

"I followed the vehicle."

"On foot?"

"I jog everyday too, remember? At least I did until this started. Besides, I only had to follow them a few blocks."

EMTs rushed down the steps to attend to the mayor, but the senator was beyond help. The two thugs against the wall who had nearly killed Ian and Jonna were also dead.

"Come on, let's get out of this basement." He led her up the steps.

"We'll have to give our statements."

"Sure. At some point. But we don't have to be here right now." He stepped from the mayor's house into the cool night air. The storm had passed and it was a muggy Florida-winter warm. Palm trees swayed in the breeze.

Visions of a different kind of experience with Jonna filled his mind.

Chin up, she remained strong, but he thought she might like to crumble after the ordeal she'd been through.

"It's over, Jonna. Three years of fear is over and done. You're safe now."

Slowly she turned her gaze to him. "You saved me, Ian. I hope you can finally forgive yourself for what happened before."

Her words warmed his heart. Yes, he thought he finally had. It was time to let that failure go and quit letting it haunt him.

"Come here." Ian drew her into his arms and held her. He wanted to hold her forever. But what now? There was no need for him to protect her anymore.

She edged away from him enough to gaze up into his face, questions in her eyes. He had questions of his own as well, but he didn't want to think about that just yet. They had survived. It was over. Jonna was safe now.

"I have to go back to Washington," she said. "I mean, after I've told them everything."

"I know." He was afraid to say more. He'd resolved he wouldn't let himself love again.

"You're good at what you do, Ian. So please don't ever give up on that. You saved my life countless times."

This was goodbye, then. Pain cracked over his heart, forming a deep fissure. He really had let her get under his skin and all the way into his heart.

Back in Washington, Jonna walked the beach. The cold wind gusted over her, and she tugged her coat tighter. The waves crashed, mesmerizing her as always. This part of the world was so different than Miami. This was her home. The Pacific Northwest and Coldwater Bay had called her back.

She didn't feel like jogging today, and needed to clear her head. How long would it take before she could get her peace of mind back?

The Oceanview Lodge sat on the cliffside—the perfect addition to the rocky coast on a stormy day. She loved the lodge and the coast. Soon she would be back inside and could warm herself by the fire.

She had good company waiting for her there too. She'd brought Aunt Debby to stay in the lodge with her for a few days. Her aunt busied herself making banana muffins for the guests while Jonna had taken a walk.

Aunt Debby claimed it was far too cold to join her. Admittedly, Jonna missed the warmth she found on the Florida beaches, but still, she preferred the rocky Washington coastline and the sound of waves hammering those rocks. That sound had lulled her to sleep on countless nights when she'd awoken from her nightmares.

But that nightmare was over.

How strange that she wished it would continue because if the danger stayed ongoing, then that would mean Ian would also remain.

He was at the lodge also, but he wouldn't be staying for long. He'd accompanied her back to Washington and to the lodge to retrieve his few belongings and his vehicle. Now that his protection duty was over, he was leaving.

Gil was expected to make a full recovery. The Shoreline Killer had been apprehended. Everything was as it should be now. So why did this weight press against her heart?

Jonna neared the lodge and saw a figure that stood at the base of the steps.

Ian. Didn't want to interrupt her contemplation? She knew what he was doing. He was waiting for her so that he could tell her that he was leaving.

Of course he would give her one last goodbye. He was good that way. Her heart ached.

She slowly approached, her gaze on the wet sand, the rocky wall next to her. Anything but Ian. She didn't want such a forlorn memory to be the last thing she associated with him—that image of him standing there, waiting to tell her farewell.

Finally, she lifted her face and took in his pensive gaze. "Did you pack your bag? Coming to say goodbye?"

Without answering, he took a step down and met her on the sand at the base of the stairs. "Uncle Gil called and offered me a new job. He wants me to come to Miami and work for him. He mentioned that he'd be reaching out to talk to you about coming back to work too."

"I'm not ever going back. I have the lodge. This is where I belong now."

"I know. I told him you would say that."

"And you? Are you going to take him up on the offer? You deserve a chance like that, you know? You're good at what you do. I wouldn't be alive now if it weren't for you. And I know I'm not easy to work with or protect."

"I won't argue with you there. I'm just glad it turned out okay and you're all right." He hesitated, frowned, then, "About Uncle Gil's offer, I'm actually hoping for a different chance," he said. "A different opportunity."

"Oh? What else have you been offered?"

"It's an offer I plan to make."

The way he looked at her made her heart leap with anticipation, but she knew she had to be mistaken. He inched even closer. "I don't want to leave, Jonna. I don't want to lose you. I can't get you out of my system. I know I haven't known you for that long, but I don't need to know you any better than I do now to be certain about how I feel. I have fallen in love with you, Jonna. Do you think you could see yourself with someone like me?"

The weight suddenly lifted from her heart, and she stepped forward and into him, pressing her lips against his as sea spray drenched them both. Through the cold, salty sea water she laughed. "Oh, Ian. I love you too. I think we're perfect together. Stay in Windsurf. Run your security-consulting business from here, but please don't offer protection services."

He kissed her back, then finally, "Only to you. I want to protect you forever, Jonna."

He got down on one knee in the sand and popped a box open. "Will you be my wife?"

Jonna's heart sputtered. She couldn't have been more surprised. But she felt no uncertainty—she knew what her answer had to be. "Yes. I wouldn't trust anyone else with the job. But…does this ring have a tracker in it?" She laughed.

"I plan to stick closer than any tracker." He grinned and kissed her tenderly. "And…I think it's high time I buy you that dinner."

* * * * *

*Don't miss the first exciting story in the
Coldwater Bay Intrigue miniseries
by Elizabeth Goddard:*

Thread of Revenge

Find more great reads at www.LoveInspired.com

Dear Reader,

Thank you for reading *Stormy Haven*. I hope you got lost in Jonna's world, stayed at her inn on the stormy coast and heard the waves crashing against the rocks, the wind wailing through the rafters. Did it give you chills? I wrapped up in blankets while I wrote the story. Ha! I had a lot of fun with these characters, Jonna and Ian. They each experienced something traumatic that had turned their worlds upside down. Each of them took a decidedly different path in order to process their experiences.

Jonna gave up her career in law enforcement to do something different with her life. Ian quit his job and became a freelance agent, but he struggled to forgive himself for past failures. Sometimes I'm reminded of my mistakes. It doesn't matter if it was a big mistake or small, I can often give in and relive my failures. That's not what God would have me do—if He can forgive me, then surely I can forgive myself. His grace is sufficient.

I hope and pray you find His grace sufficient, and trust that in times of trouble, He will set you upon a rock—He will be your refuge. A safe haven, rather than a stormy haven.

I love to connect with my readers. Please be sure to visit my website—ElizabethGoddard.com—to find ways to connect, and to sign up for my Great Escapes Newsletter.

Many blessings,
Elizabeth Goddard

COMING NEXT MONTH FROM
Love Inspired® Suspense

Available October 2, 2018

BATTLE TESTED
Military K-9 Unit • by Laura Scott

Former air force pilot Isaac Goddard's only goal is to bring his late friend's dog home from combat—until he stumbles across an attack on nurse Vanessa Gomez. With the Red Rose Killer determined to make Vanessa his next victim, Isaac vows to guard her at all costs.

UNDERCOVER MEMORIES
by Lenora Worth

After waking up in the hospital, private investigator Emma Langston knows she was sent on an urgent case—but she can't remember her mission. Now someone wants her dead, and her only chance of surviving long enough to recover her memories is by relying on Detective Ryder Palladin for protection.

AMISH CHRISTMAS SECRETS
Amish Protectors • by Debby Giusti

When a man shows up at the nursing home where Amish single mother Rosie Glick works, demanding incriminating evidence her murdered boyfriend stole, Ezra Stoltz comes to her rescue. But with the killer dead set on silencing Rosie, Ezra must hide her and her baby to keep them safe.

IN TOO DEEP
by Sharon Dunn

After one of the at-risk teens she mentors calls her for help, Sierra Monforton witnesses a drug deal and becomes a target. And while undercover DEA agent Joseph Anderson's assignment is to take down a drug ring, he'll risk everything—including blowing his cover—to ensure Sierra doesn't get hurt.

GRAVE PERIL
by Mary Alford

Jamie Hendricks always believed her late father was innocent of murder... and now her uncle claims to have proof. Only CIA agent Gavin Dalton—her ex-boyfriend and the son of her father's supposed victim—can help her uncover a deadly conspiracy that goes deeper than anyone expected.

FRAMED FOR CHRISTMAS
by Jaycee Bullard

Someone's framing DNA technician Dani Jones for drug smuggling— and they plan to kill her to cover the truth. Can former DEA agent Gideon Marshall and his retired drug-sniffing dog make sure she survives long enough to find out why...and clear her name?

LOOK FOR THESE AND OTHER LOVE INSPIRED BOOKS WHEREVER BOOKS ARE SOLD, INCLUDING MOST BOOKSTORES, SUPERMARKETS, DISCOUNT STORES AND DRUGSTORES.

LISCNM0918

Get 4 FREE REWARDS!

We'll send you 2 FREE Books plus 2 FREE Mystery Gifts.

Love Inspired® Suspense books feature Christian characters facing challenges to their faith... and lives.

FREE
Value Over
$20

YES! Please send me 2 FREE Love Inspired® Suspense novels and my 2 FREE mystery gifts (gifts are worth about $10 retail). After receiving them, if I don't wish to receive any more books, I can return the shipping statement marked "cancel." If I don't cancel, I will receive 4 brand-new novels every month and be billed just $5.24 each for the regular-print edition or $5.74 each for the larger-print edition in the U.S., or $5.74 each for the regular-print edition or $6.24 each for the larger-print edition in Canada. That's a savings of at least 13% off the cover price. It's quite a bargain! Shipping and handling is just 50¢ per book in the U.S. and 75¢ per book in Canada*. I understand that accepting the 2 free books and gifts places me under no obligation to buy anything. I can always return a shipment and cancel at any time. The free books and gifts are mine to keep no matter what I decide.

Choose one: ☐ **Love Inspired® Suspense
Regular-Print**
(153/353 IDN GMY5)

☐ **Love Inspired® Suspense
Larger-Print**
(107/307 IDN GMY5)

Name (please print)

Address   Apt. #

City   State/Province   Zip/Postal Code

Mail to the **Reader Service:**
IN U.S.A.: P.O. Box 1341, Buffalo, NY 14240-8531
IN CANADA: P.O. Box 603, Fort Erie, Ontario L2A 5X3

Want to try two free books from another series! Call 1-800-873-8635 or visit www.ReaderService.com.

---

*Terms and prices subject to change without notice. Prices do not include applicable taxes. Sales tax applicable in N.Y. Canadian residents will be charged applicable taxes. Offer not valid in Quebec. This offer is limited to one order per household. Books received may not be as shown. Not valid for current subscribers to Love Inspired Suspense books. All orders subject to approval. Credit or debit balances in a customer's account(s) may be offset by any other outstanding balance owed by or to the customer. Please allow 4 to 6 weeks for delivery. Offer available while quantities last.

Your Privacy—The Reader Service is committed to protecting your privacy. Our Privacy Policy is available online at www.ReaderService.com or upon request from the Reader Service. We make a portion of our mailing list available to reputable third parties that offer products we believe may interest you. If you prefer that we not exchange your name with third parties, or if you wish to clarify or modify your communication preferences, please visit us at www.ReaderService.com/consumerschoice or write to us at Reader Service Preference Service, P.O. Box 9062, Buffalo, NY 14240-9062. Include your complete name and address.

LIS18

Looking for inspiration in tales
of hope, faith and heartfelt romance?

Check out **Love Inspired**® and
Love Inspired® **Suspense** books!

New books available every month!

CONNECT WITH US AT:

Harlequin.com/Community

 Facebook.com/HarlequinBooks

 Twitter.com/HarlequinBooks

 Instagram.com/HarlequinBooks

 Pinterest.com/HarlequinBooks

ReaderService.com

LIGENRE2018